Jade's Story

Helena Pielichaty

D1099389

OXFORD
UNIVERSITY PRESS

OXFORD
UNIVERSITY PRESS

Great Clarendon Street, Oxford OX2 6DP

Oxford University Press is a department of the University of Oxford.
It furthers the University's objective of excellence in research, scholarship,
and education by publishing worldwide in

Oxford New York

Athens Auckland Bangkok Bogotá Buenos Aires Cape Town
Chennai Dar es Salaam Delhi Florence Hong Kong Istanbul Karachi
Kolkata Kuala Lumpur Madrid Melbourne Mexico City Mumbai Nairobi
Paris São Paulo Shanghai Singapore Taipei Tokyo Toronto Warsaw

with associated companies in Berlin Ibadan

Oxford is a registered trade mark of Oxford University Press
in the UK and in certain other countries

British Library Cataloguing in Publication Data available

ISBN 0 19 275164 6

1 3 5 7 9 10 8 6 4 2

Typeset by AFS Image Setters Ltd, Glasgow

Printed in Great Britain by
Cox & Wyman Ltd, Reading, Berkshire

Acknowledgements

*To Justin Schlicht and Elaine Bowerman for their tremendous
help and insight
To Lesley Philips at Newark MIND and the staff at Bassetlaw
Hospital for giving me their time and advice
To Linda Jennings and Gwen Grant for helping me choose the
first chapter when I was stuck*

*This book is dedicated to my sister Tanya
and brothers David and Mark,
with love*

1

It was a blistering hot Friday afternoon. Even with every window and door wide open the classroom was stifling. Everything was an effort and Mr Cooper had decided silent reading was about as much as his Year Six class could take before the special assembly. 'Get out a book and wallow in it,' he instructed, sinking down into his captain's chair to finish off the last chapter of *Bumface*.

Jade Winter didn't feel like wallowing. Instead, she scribbled a message and passed it across to her friend, Rosemarie. 'Hi, Rosie. It's me,' she put.

'Hi, me.'

'I'm bored.'

'I'm hot.'

'I'm hot and bored.'

'I'm bored and hot.'

'Is this a poem?'

'Is that a question?'

'Is this an answer?'

'Stop it.'

'No.'

'Yes.'

'No.'

'I bet you get the trophy,' Rosie continued.

Jade scowled in disbelief. 'So likely!' she replied.

'You will.'

'*You* will.'

'I don't think so. Not with my handicaps.'

'??????'

'Look across.'

Jade looked. On the other side of the room, Rosie's twin brother, Navid, was picking his nose with one hand while turning the pages of *Where Babies Come From* with the other. From time to time he would shake his head in wonder, either at the contents of the book or the contents of his nose. Who knew?

'See what you mean,' Jade wrote.

'You're going to win the trophy.'

Jade shrugged, as if it didn't matter to her either way. 'It'll probably go to someone in Miss Seger's. They're all boffy.'

'Yeah.'

'Yeah.'

Finally, the bell went for last break. There was an immediate outburst of chair scraping and book slamming and noise. Coolly, Mr Cooper set down his book, then folded his arms and waited, his face expressionless. There was instant silence. His class knew that otherwise he would start counting and that whatever number he reached meant the number of seconds they had to stay in the classroom during break. It was too hot for all that today.

He was on the verge of dismissing them when he frowned. 'I've forgotten something,' he said, glancing sideways at his desk. 'What have I forgotten?'

'The letters about the Leavers' Service,' Jade replied straightaway. 'They're the yellow ones there,' she said, pointing.

Mr Cooper smacked his hand against his forehead. 'You, Jade Winter, are a wonderful person. If I'd forgotten to give them out again Mrs Gamgee would have had my guts for garters.'

Jade smiled, allowing the praise to ripple warmly through her.

'Creep,' Navid muttered lightly from behind as they lined up to collect their copies before escaping into the playground.

The two top classes filed noisily into the hall for assembly, nudging each other, indifferent to the Year Three recorder group. They were going to hear who had won what in this year's prize-giving and no tragic rendition of 'London's Burning' was going to distract them.

As soon as the music had finished, Mrs Gamgee strode up in her crumpled linen suit, a wide beam on her face. 'Wasn't that marvellous?' she asked, leading the applause.

'Yeah—if you're deaf,' Navid mumbled from the safety of the back row. Jade elbowed him in the ribs.

Mrs Gamgee sighed heavily and shook her tightly permed head. 'I can't believe it's the end of the year in two weeks. Two weeks! And with so much to get through—Sports Day next week, the Leavers' Service and disco the week after. Hands up if you're coming to the disco?'

Virtually every hand was raised. 'I thought so!' Mrs Gamgee enthused. 'I'm looking forward to shaking a leg with the Year Six boys!'

'She's not shaking anything near me, the pervert!' Navid whispered as the younger pupils turned to stare and mock.

'And hands up if you're coming to the Leavers' Service?' Mrs Gamgee asked.

This was a trick question as only the older pupils were invited, so only they raised their hands. This was followed by another theatrical shake of the tight perm. 'Tch! It doesn't seem two minutes since you were all in nursery class throwing sand at each other and eating worms.'

'Like that really happened,' Navid hissed in Jade's ear.

Jade pretended not to have heard. There was never a dull moment with Navid but there were times when she wished he would stop being the wise-guy and just listen.

Unconsciously, she reached for a strand of her hair and began to suck the ends as Mrs Gamgee explained the importance of the Leavers' Service to the rest of the school. 'And this,' Mrs Gamgee eventually announced, 'is what every Year Six pupil will receive from Lorimer Lane as a unique memento of their time with us.'

A colourful piece of card was held up, its detail impossible to see from the back, but Jade knew exactly what it was. The Leaving Certificate. She knew all about them because her father, Goran Winter, wrote them.

He was a calligrapher, who owned a specialist pen and stationery shop on Trafalgar Road called Inks. Every year, he painstakingly filled in the details of each school leaver's achievements in his beautiful italic hand. They took him a long time—too long, her mother said, considering he did them for free.

Usually, the certificates were less colourful than the one Mrs Gamgee was displaying, and Jade stopped sucking her hair for a moment in order to concentrate.

'They're a bit different this year,' Mrs Gamgee confirmed, as if reading Jade's mind. 'I've had them especially printed, with the achievement, and the school name and logo already done. They're really bright, aren't they? All we need now are the names.'

There was an immediate shuffling and raising of tension at the back of the hall but Jade's eyes focused worriedly on the new-style certificate, not taking in anything Mrs Gamgee said. What would her dad think about the change? He'd been even moodier than normal lately. This wouldn't help.

A punch on her arm from Rosemarie brought her back to the present. Mrs Gamgee had swapped the certificate for the trophy. This was the big one. Only one Year Six pupil—and there were seventy-two of them this time—received the additional award for Outstanding Contribution to the School. It was hard to win and everyone wanted to win it—if not for the fancy shield then definitely for the fifty pound gift voucher that came with it.

The shield was held high for them all to see. 'I'm going to announce the name of the Year Six who will be only the fourth person to receive this trophy,' Mrs Gamgee announced solemnly. 'Last year, it went to Joey Vaesen. As you know, Joey was an amazing athlete—I don't think his name's been out of the sports pages of the *Evening Post* since he left. This year, though, the award goes to someone who has contributed to the school in a very different way. This person isn't particularly brilliant at sport or schoolwork . . . '

'That's me out, then,' Navid grumbled.

' . . . but has consistently given to the school in a vitally important way. This person is reliable, hard-working, well-mannered and, above all, puts others first. This person has turned up to every after-school activity to set out the chairs or help with refreshments or sell raffle tickets.' Mrs Gamgee paused. 'Put your hand up if you think you know who I'm talking about,' she said.

'It could be you!' Navid hissed at Jade in his 'Lottery winners' voice as several hands shot into the air.

Jade shook her head. 'No way,' she hissed back, but her heart was beating rapidly.

The headteacher smiled, then continued. 'This person has a one hundred per cent attendance record, collects all the dinner registers for Mrs Fell every morning and is in charge of the tuck shop at break . . . '

Jade buried her head in her hands, her heart beating so rapidly now against her polo shirt she thought it would explode.

' . . . it is, of course, Mr Cooper's "Little Gem", Jade Winter!' Mrs Gamgee ended triumphantly.

Slowly, Jade looked up, her face a deep crimson suffused with a mixture of embarrassment and pride. Her eyes slid to where Mr Cooper was sitting. He stopped clapping long enough to give her a 'thumbs up'. It was the best moment of her life.

After assembly, she collected the box of certificates from Mrs Gamgee's office to take home for her father to complete, as she did every year. 'You don't mind, do you, Jade? I know it's a bit different this time,' the headteacher beamed.

'I don't mind,' Jade replied, still dazed from the news.

'The list of names and awards is in an envelope down the side. If he could have them ready by the end of next week I'd be grateful.'

'OK.'

'I'm sure he'll be pleased with them—they shouldn't take him half as long now.'

'No,' Jade agreed warily. So *that* was the whole purpose behind the trendy new designs. Speed. Her father was always very last minute with things. The certificates had only been completed on the day of the service last year. *Well, she got them, didn't she?* her father had shrugged when Jade had complained.

A look of understanding crossed between pupil and teacher. 'They'll be on time,' Jade promised.

'You're a poppet.'

Chattering loudly, the trio left Lorimer Lane and crossed onto the busier Albert Street. 'I knew you'd win. I told you!' Rosemarie said as she relieved Jade of her schoolbag by passing it straight on to Navid.

Jade blushed. 'I still can't believe it!'

'Fifty quid,' Navid groaned. 'Fifty quid! I hope you're *not* going to spend it wisely.'

'No, I'm going to throw it in the bin.'

'Which bin?' Navid asked as he tried to steal the list from the box. Thwarted, he turned his attention to the vast Computer Heaven warehouse across the street. 'That's where I'd spend it—every penny. I'd get that new *Kick Boxer* CD-Rom and *3-D clip-art* and . . .'

He broke off to try to beat Rosemarie to pressing the button at the pedestrian crossing. 'What about you? What would you get?' he asked Jade.

'Nothing from there.'

'Why not? It's miles better than anywhere else. I'd live there if I could. Well, there or Elland Road.'

The appearance of the green man saved her having to explain. Quickly, she crossed the road and dashed ahead. They were close to Inks now and she hoped her father wouldn't see her walking past the window. She could invite Nav and Rosie back to the flat upstairs then without him knowing. If she had to ask, he'd shrug his permission begrudgingly but keep shouting up, asking what time they were going, spoiling the visit. Or worse, come out with one of those odd comments or do something that made her want to curl up and die. Nobody ever said anything but sometimes she caught her friends exchanging looks, as if to say, 'What's *he* on?'

But there was no need to sneak past today. Inks was closed, its windows firmly obscured by cold, vandal-proof shutters. Jade blinked, the box in her arms suddenly weighing heavily. 'How come it's shut?' Rosie asked.

'I don't know,' Jade replied.

'I'm dropping in next door to see if there's any free samples going,' Navid stated.

Jade glanced from the forbidding steel panels of Inks

to the neighbouring freshly painted shop front of Krazinski's Continental Bakery. 'Yeah, let's,' she agreed readily.

Jacob Krazinski, the old Polish owner, was a favourite among the local children. As soft as his bread cakes, he was always good for some treat or other; broken biscuits, over-baked tarts, misshapen rolls—as long as the children asked politely. He couldn't abide rudeness.

Inside the shop, Jacob grinned at the three new customers through tannin-stained teeth. 'So, another day of education over, hah?' he asked.

Navid pointed to Jade. 'Winter's won the Outstanding Award for the school. She's a right boff-head.'

Jacob scratched his double chin and gazed fondly at the girl. 'The Outstanding Award? For what you have to do this? Stand outside? In all weathers? Rain or shine? Hale and Pace?'

The children looked at him, to check whether he was being serious or not. Even after over fifty years in England, his English could be a little wobbly at times. But the grin gave him away. 'It is good, this award?'

'Oh, yeah,' Rosie said, 'it's dead good to win it.'

'You get fifty quid,' Navid added, 'and she's giving me half for being her best mate, aren't you?'

But Jade was not listening. Her eyes were turned to the open door, flicking keenly from one passer-by to the next, like a zealous customs officer at an airport. 'Do you know what time Dad closed the shop, Jacob?' she asked lightly, her eyes still fixed on the entrance.

'He did not open today, at all, I think,' Jacob replied.

'Oh.' Jade shrugged her shoulders and hoisted the box higher. 'He's probably at the suppliers.'

'Sure,' said Jacob. 'You have key to get in?'

The girl nodded. Her two friends gathered their bags and began to follow her out.

'It's OK,' she said, 'I can manage.'

A look of pain crossed Rosie's face and she leaned over and whispered urgently in Jade's ear. 'Oh, all right,' Jade agreed, 'but you'll have to ignore the flat if it's messy.'

'I live with Navid,' Rosie stated equably as she sidled past her brother, who was doing a good sucking-up job on Jacob's skills as a baker.

Mr Krazinski glanced regretfully at the assorted remains of fresh cream doughnuts and Danish pastries in his cabinet. 'You come back in half an hour. I give you outstanding cakes for outstanding students.'

Navid checked his watch. 'Roger that. Outstanding cakes at seventeen hundred hours. Over.'

The amused baker waved the boy away. 'Cheeky kid,' he chortled.

Jade led the way down the passage and along the backs of the row of shops. She kneed open the creosote gate, weaving between the dozens of terracotta planters full of vibrant flowers, and clanked up the fire-escape.

At the top, Jade tried the door, hoping it would be locked. Let him be out. Let him be out. Let him be out, she muttered to herself. But the door yielded easily and her stomach lurched.

Inside, it was dark and stuffy. The kitchen curtains were still drawn, as were the ones on the landing. Jade drew them back sharply, squinting as the sun flooded greedily through. Rosie dashed to the bathroom at the end of the passageway while Navid dropped the bags by the telephone table. 'I'll just put this in the front room,' Jade said. 'Hang on here.'

The front room was dark and gloomy, too; the Victorian wooden shutters blocking out any chance of light or sun.

Jade had hoped to leave the box on the table unnoticed but her father's voice found her. 'Who's that?' he asked tiredly from his chair in the corner.

'Only me,' Jade replied.

He mumbled something and she stepped forward to look at him. Her heart sank. Navid and Rosie must not be allowed to see him. No way.

2

Jade knew that with someone like Navid in the house she had little chance of privacy. 'God, it's like the inside of Darth Vader's underpants in here,' the boy burst out cheerfully. He peered into the shadows. 'Oh, hiya, Mr Winter. Didn't see you. How you doing?'

There was no answer. 'It's Navid, Dad, and Rosie. They've just popped in—they're not staying,' Jade explained hastily.

'I am,' Navid contradicted, 'I've got to wait till Jacob gives us some buns.'

Mr Winter muttered something neither child could hear properly.

'Tell him, then, Jadey. Tell him the news, super star,' Navid continued.

'No,' Jade said sharply, adding in a whisper, 'not yet. I want to wait until Mum comes home and tell them together.'

'Got you—sozz,' Nav apologized in his version of a whisper.

'What? What are you saying? What are you doing?' Jade's father asked, his voice low and petulant.

'Nothing,' Jade said quickly, tugging Navid's arm, 'we're going to get a drink.'

'Then send the vermin home,' Mr Winter muttered as Jade closed the door behind her.

In the kitchen, she hurriedly filled three glasses with Vimto while Navid went to heckle his sister for taking so long. 'Come on, metal mouth! Have you got your big butt stuck or something?' Jade heard him ask. She wished Jacob hadn't promised free cakes in half an hour. Half an hour was too long to have people in the house when Dad was like this, on one of his 'downers'. He'd had them before, these dark moods, and by the look of him he was sinking fast into this one. Witnesses were definitely not wanted.

Rosie flounced into the kitchen ahead of her brother, firing dirty looks at him. 'Can't even go to the loo in peace,' she complained.

'You didn't go to the loo, you murdered it! It stinks!' Navid said, pinching his nose with his fingers.

'You've some room to talk, anyway, Haldijary. I saw you picking your nose and eating it during silent reading,' Jade teased.

'Bogies are free, home-grown, and don't need cooking, so what's the problem?' Navid answered flatly. They all burst out laughing.

'What's this?' a voice asked.

Jade's face reddened as her father appeared in front of them, one hand on the kitchen table to steady himself, the other clutching one of the new certificates. He looked in such a state with his hair sticking up at all angles like a mad professor's and his eyes glazed and staring, as if he were drunk, though Jade knew he wasn't. Worse, he hadn't even bothered to get dressed—he was still in pyjamas and *then* his pyjama jacket was buttoned wrongly so that his head and neck looked oddly angled, like some grotesque life-size puppet's. Rosie and Navid must be thinking all sorts.

'What's this?' he repeated, holding up the certificates.

'They're the new certificates,' Jade explained, her voice wavering slightly.

'Cool, aren't they?' Navid said. 'Will you do mine first? Put "to the King".'

12

The calligrapher emitted a shuddering gasp, like an angry horse irritated by flies. All of a sudden, tears began to fall freely and rapidly down his whiskered cheeks. He made no attempt to hide them, or wipe them away. Hastily, Jade tore a section of kitchen roll for Goran but he did not take it. She hesitated, not wanting to do it for him, but feeling she had little choice when mucus and spittle began to mingle with the tears, so extreme was the outburst.

The more sensitive Rosie turned away. 'It's that flu,' she said to Navid. 'Mum had it, remember.'

'Yeah,' Navid agreed doubtfully, glancing sideways at the spectacle, 'it didn't make her roar, though.'

'No, we leave that to you,' Rosie said sarcastically before addressing Jade's father. 'You need to get to bed, Mr Winter, and take loads of paracetamol.'

He stared at her for a second, his eyes pink and bloodshot. 'Useless,' he sobbed. 'I'm just useless.'

Jade attempted to guide her father out of the kitchen and away from them but he was strong, and his arm seemed to be riveted to the table. 'Why?' he kept repeating. 'Why?'

'Hey,' said Navid suddenly, 'it's bun time!'

'Will you be all right?' Rosie asked Jade.

'Sure, you go,' Jade reassured her, too humiliated to meet her friend's gaze. 'You'd better be quick, too. It's shabat—Jacob won't hang around.'

Navid didn't need telling a second time. He scooped his bags from the hallway. 'See you Monday, Jade, see you, Mr Winter. Hope you get better.'

'Paracetamol,' Rosie repeated, following her brother, 'and barley water. Barley water's really good.'

Jade nodded. Barley water. If only.

Once the twins had left, Goran shuffled back to his chair in the front room, taking the certificates with him.

Jade closed the door to the front room and called her mother at work.

It seemed to take an age for the switchboard operators at the university to answer and even longer to connect her to Ruth Winter's administration department. Jade knew summer was the busiest time, with old students calling for results and new students calling for details about accommodation and grants and a million other things. When Ruth did at last answer, Jade could only blurt out what had happened in one long, agitated sentence. ' . . . and he cried right in front of them,' she concluded miserably.

Ruth listened patiently, her voice calm and soothing. 'OK. OK. I'll be home as soon as I can. Daddy's just a bit stressed at the moment. I told him not to open the shop if he didn't feel up to it.'

'If you say so,' Jade replied.

'I do. Just make him a cup of tea if he wants one, otherwise give him space, all right? I'd better go. I'll bring pizza home with me, OK? Love you.'

'Love you.'

Jade sat on her bed, chewing her hair, waiting for Ruth to come home. Worrying. Should she call Rosie and ask her not to say anything at school on Monday? Or would that make things worse? What if Navid, blabbermouth that he was, told everyone about her dad crying? She couldn't stand the embarrassment if he did. Jade sucked harder on her saturated hair, wishing she had someone to talk to about her problem. About how you cope when your dad's weird.

When Ruth arrived, she persuaded Goran to go for a bath, then read a book. He obeyed without argument, as if he were an unassuming hotel guest, grateful for direction.

Later, as her mother dried the dishes and Jade washed, she explained his behaviour away in hushed tones. 'He hasn't been sleeping properly and tiredness makes people over-emotional. That lousy Computer Heaven has taken most of our stationery trade since Christmas. It's hard enough for small businesses to survive on the outskirts of town without megastores opening opposite you and rubbing your nose in it. That's what's triggered this.'

'But they sell computers not fountain pens, don't they?' Jade asked. This was just a guess. Her father had forbidden her to even look through the warehouse window, let alone go in.

'Yes, but how many people do you know who use fountain pens? They're not exactly top of the consumer list. It was the paper and envelopes the local office staff used to buy from us that kept us afloat but it's half the price over there,' Ruth replied.

'Mr Cooper does,' Jade said.

'Does what?'

'Use a fountain pen. It's a tortoiseshell barrel with real ink, not cartridges.'

'He's a dying breed, I'm afraid. It's a good thing I'm on a reasonable salary because if trade doesn't buck up soon we might have to close the shop—but don't tell your grandma, whatever you do.'

Jade nodded. Grandma didn't get on with her dad at the best of times. Telling her this wouldn't help, especially as it had been her grandma Sheila's money that had helped them to buy Inks in the first place—a fact she never tired of reminding them of.

'OK, I won't, but . . . but why did Dad have to cry? Men don't cry, do they?' Jade asked.

Her mother smiled down at her, wagging the tea towel under her nose. 'That's a bit sexist! Don't you ever watch football?'

Jade shrugged. Maybe it was sexist. It didn't matter so much now, anyway. It was the weekend and Ruth would be here to sort everything out. Let Goran sit in a chair all day if he wanted to, as long as there were no outsiders to see and hear him, what did it matter? Resolutely, she plunged her hand into the suddy water and fished for another pot to wash.

'So, how was school anyway? Only two weeks at primary left. I can't believe it!' Ruth clucked.

'You sound like Mrs Gamgee,' Jade began, then dropped the cup she had been about to pass to her mother.

'Butter fingers!' Ruth admonished, catching it just in time.

'I've just remembered!' Jade cried. 'I've got something to tell you.'

Had Jade wanted to phone Rosie that evening, she would have had to use the box on the end of Trafalgar Road. The Winters' phone was constantly engaged, with Ruth calling one person after another to boast about her daughter's achievement. Over an hour was spent with Grandma alone, with Jade having to explain in minute detail about the trophy. 'And you won it over seventy-two others, you say?' Grandma asked.

'Well, it's not really a competition, Grandma,' Jade tried to explain.

'Seventy-two. Oh, just wait till I tell them at Weight Watchers,' she replied smugly.

Jade rolled her eyes at her mother, who rolled hers in return.

'And I'll be adding to that money,' Grandma continued. 'I'd planned to give you something for starting at the High School anyway.'

'Thanks, Grandma. See you Sunday. Do you want to talk to Mum again?'

'Yes, she can help me work out the wording for the *Evening Post*.'

'Grandma, no!' Jade pleaded.

'But I'm so proud of you.'

'I'll be in the paper anyway with school next week. They'll think I'm a right swell-head if you put me in too.'

'All right, Trouble,' Grandma conceded. 'Just let me know what day so I can tell everyone to buy a copy—and I might even treat you to pavlova when you come to lunch.'

'Ohh, Grandma, think of the calories,' Jade teased.

By the end of the night the only person who hadn't congratulated her was Goran, who spent the evening staring miserably at the box on the table, muttering to himself.

3

Goran didn't emerge from the bedroom at all the next day. Ruth opened Inks, as Jade had guessed she would.

Jade spent the day with her mother, tidying the shelves, bringing fresh stock from the back, opening the door for the few customers they had. When no one was in the shop, Jade tried out the exclusive pens from the special cabinet, gently prising them, one at a time, from their satin beds. Goran would never have allowed it, but Ruth didn't mind her 'test driving', as long as she was careful. Her favourite was a fat-barrelled lapis-lazuli effect Waterman. She imagined herself in posh clothes shops signing cheques with it, or using it to write ream after ream in a leather-bound journal.

After lunch a woman placed an order for hand-written place settings and menu cards for her daughter's wedding. 'We've heard Mr Winter's italic's lovely,' she explained.

'His copperplate's excellent as well,' Ruth informed her.

Automatically, Jade fetched the laminated calligraphy samples from one of the shelves. 'It says ''The quick brown fox jumps over the lazy dog'' because that covers every letter of the alphabet,' she explained as they studied the sheets.

The customer gave her an 'oh, how cute' smile and looked impressed, eventually placing an order for italic lettering in Royal Blue ink on cream vellum card 'to match the bridesmaids' dresses'.

18

Jade felt a surge of pride as Ruth took down details and arranged to call them with a quote the following week. 'Can I go tell Dad? It might cheer him up?' Jade asked, knowing anything to do with calligraphy was what Goran called 'real' work, as opposed to serving customers which 'any imbecile' could do.

But the news did not please him, as she had hoped. 'I don't care,' he muttered, pulling the duvet higher. 'I need peace.'

'He needs peace,' Jade informed her mother.

'Don't we all,' Ruth replied, frowning into the empty till.

On Sunday, they managed to persuade Goran to have breakfast with them. Jade fetched the papers while her mother set the table in the front room. 'These get heavier,' Jade moaned as she dropped the mixture of tabloids and broadsheets onto the chair.

'I know—all those trees,' Ruth said, depositing a basket of warmed croissants next to the teapot, 'but you can't beat a lazy Sunday morning with the *News of the World*.'

'It's disgusting though—look at that woman on the front—all her boobs are hanging out.'

'Oh, you just ignore those bits.'

'How can I—they're enormous!' Jade exclaimed.

Ruth swiftly heaved out *The Sunday Times* from the bottom of the pile and whacked it on top of the offending picture. 'Better?' she asked.

'Much,' Jade sniffed piously, rummaging for the *Funday* section.

Goran shuffled in, scowling at the brightness of the room.

'How are you feeling?' Ruth asked softly, pulling

out a chair so her husband could sit next to her. He sat awkwardly, as if his body were unused to bending, and looked bewildered by the array of food in front of him.

Jade thought what a contrast her parents made. First, her mother, small and slim with freckly brown arms that never stayed still, dressed in a sleeveless summer dress that made her look young and pretty. Then next to her slumped her father, gaunt and bedraggled, his shoulders rounded as if shielding himself from an icy wind. It irked her to see him like this. He could have made an effort, couldn't he, after all his time in bed? Surely he couldn't still be tired?

'Do you want the jam, Dad?' she asked, holding out the glass dish towards him. 'It's Grandma's home-made stuff.'

Goran stared suspiciously at the plump strawberries bulging through the rich syrup. 'Maggots,' he said.

'Mum uses a spray on her soft fruits, Goran. The jam's delicious,' Ruth said calmly.

'No. No food. Just tea.'

'I'll do it,' Jade offered. Carefully, she poured the hot liquid into a cup, added plenty of sugar before passing it to her father.

'Thank you,' he said.

'Do you know what's worse than finding a maggot in your dinner?' Jade asked. She paused. She had told this one a million times before but her mother smiled gamely, encouraging her to continue. 'Finding half a maggot!' she finished.

'Oh, *please*!' Ruth protested.

Goran said nothing, frowning instead at the open window, then grimacing as a lorry passed, making the glass rattle. Jade sensed her father's growing irritation and discomfort and became wary. She ate her cereal slowly, concentrating on the woody specks of wheat which floated in the milk.

'Oh no,' Ruth sighed from behind *The Sunday Times,* 'that's dreadful.'

'What is?' Jade asked.

'They've found another mass grave in Kosovo. Three hundred people, mainly women and children. Look Goran.' Ruth pointed out the article which dominated the front page. Jade knew her father had been following the war in Kosovo all year, staring anxiously at the television set and watching out for every bulletin as it came in. He never passed an opinion or discussed the events, just watched, transfixed. He had come from one of the countries near there called Bosnia but he never talked about it if she asked, so she had stopped asking. Besides, the *News* was so boring, especially war news, in places miles away nobody had even heard of.

'It's like Hitler all over again,' Ruth continued heatedly.

'Show me,' Goran said, reaching across the table for the paper. At first, he scowled as he skimmed the page but then the scowl changed into a snarl and finally laughter. Laughter that loosened his rounded shoulders but set Jade's teeth on edge. She looked at her mother, puzzled, waiting for an explanation.

Ruth stared sorrowfully at her husband before helping him up. 'Come on,' she stated firmly, 'back to bed.'

Jade glanced at the photograph of mutilated bodies piled like cheap clothing in a jumble sale and wondered how anyone could find that *funny*. She told her grandma about it, when she phoned to cancel their afternoon visit. Sheila Winter sniffed, not beginning to hide her disdain for her son-in-law. 'Frankly, nothing that man does surprises me,' she said flatly, 'but that's foreigners for you.'

At least Jade had school, her haven. The first thing Rosie did on Monday was enquire how Goran was, allowing Jade to shrug and say that yes, he had the flu, thanks for asking. Navid then described the 'wickedness' of the buns she had missed and that was that. They neither asked to call in on the way home nor questioned the closed shop-front as they waved goodbye. Jade relaxed, separating home from school without a qualm, as she always had. Besides, there was plenty to do. Projects to finish. Rehearsals for the Leavers' Service. Sports Day. Before she knew it, it was Friday again and Jade Winter had only one week left as a Year Six.

At breaktime, she had been asked to wait by the entrance with Navid to greet two visitors to the school. Mr Cooper had arranged for students from the High School to come and answer questions about life there, or as he put it, *The Head Down The Bog Talk*. 'I don't want to leave Lorimer Lane,' Jade confessed.

'What? High School's going to be wicked, man. I can't wait!' Navid replied, licking the inside of his crisp packet.

'It won't have Mr Cooper, though, will it?' Jade replied.

'Good,' retorted Navid, 'he's still got five yoyos of mine he nicked.'

'Confiscated for using them as deadly weapons, dork,' Jade reminded him.

'Whatever. Oh-oh. Pervert alert.'

Jade looked up to see Mrs Gamgee heading towards them. 'She's not a pervert,' Jade admonished.

'I know, I just like saying it,' Navid admitted.

'Are the certificates nearly ready, Jade?' Mrs Gamgee asked without preamble.

'Oh yeah, they'll be ready Monday,' Jade replied, swallowing hard.

The headmistress nodded, continuing on her way. 'Excellent, excellent.'

'Excellent, excellent,' Navid imitated before letting out a low growl, 'ex-ce-llent!' he growled in admiration.

Jade followed his gaze to where the two High School students were bent over the signing-in book. 'She's not all *that* good,' Jade sniffed as she surveyed the long golden hair of the female student.

'I knew all that sex reading would come in useful one day,' Navid whispered, leaping up to open the doors.

Mr Cooper's class had Thomas, much to Navid's disgust. 'No, no one has ever shoved my head down the toilet!' the Year Eleven confirmed.

'Pity,' Navid whispered to Jade, 'he looks as if he could do with a wash.'

'Shh, Nav, it's important,' Jade whispered back, keen to hear what else the visitor had to say about the High School. It was all right for Navid—he had brothers and sisters there already; someone to watch out for him in September, as well as Rosie. She hadn't. She needed to know as much as possible. If she *had* to leave Lorimer Lane she might as well know what she was letting herself in for.

Mr Cooper put his hand up to ask a question. The Y11 grinned. 'Yes, Mr Cooper?'

'I think everything you've said this afternoon has been brilliant, Tom, but if you had one piece of advice to give to the class about secondary school, what would it be?'

Tom looked thoughtful. 'That it's a fresh start, I suppose. No one judges you on what you've done

23

here—good or bad. You're starting again with a clean slate.'

Mr Cooper nodded in agreement. 'I think that's a really important point. You *are* being given the chance for a fresh start; a chance to impress.'

'I'll impress them the minute I walk in the joint,' Navid bragged loudly.

'You'll impress me if you even find the joint!' his sister rejoined.

'Enough, enough,' Mr Cooper commanded good-humouredly before thanking Tom for coming in. 'It's been really useful. I'm sure they've learned a lot.'

'Cheers, Mr C. See you all next year,' Tom smiled before gathering his belongings and going to collect his partner from Miss Seger's.

Jade stared after him, finding it hard to believe she would ever look so grown-up and be so confident.

After school she dragged her feet, not wanting to go home. Ruth wouldn't be back until six and her father was . . . her father was her father. *Bit different from last week*, she thought to herself, remembering how elated she had been.

'Good evening, Miss Winter. You look as if you lost a penny and found a pound,' Jacob greeted from his doorway. She smiled weakly at him, too tired to correct his mistake.

Upstairs, Jade dropped her bag and entered the front room. She knew it would be dark and that her father would be either asleep or just sitting in the corner, muttering to himself. She hoped he would be asleep. She could at least have the TV on then, even if she did have to turn the sound off. 'Who's that?' Goran asked suspiciously from his corner.

'Me,' she said, automatically glancing at the box of certificates on the table. 'Oh, you've done them!' she exclaimed, seeing the box lid had been tightly sealed with grey elephant tape—always a sign that the job had been completed. 'Oh, Dad, thanks! That's brilliant! Mrs Gamgee asked me again today and I told her Monday and it will be Monday! Thanks!' Overjoyed, she dashed to the corner to hug him. He didn't respond to her embrace, but then he never did.

'He's getting better, Mum, look,' Jade announced as soon as Ruth came home from work. Her mother glanced from the box to her husband's morose face and nodded.

'I hope so,' she stated.

'I was getting dead worried in case I had to tell Mrs Gamgee he hadn't done the certificates but now I don't have to.'

'No,' Ruth replied distractedly, moving across to the television set.

'We had two students in school today telling us about the High. Navid wanted the girl and went into a right strop because we had Tom instead,' Jade continued. Ruth crouched down behind the set as Jade chatted on. 'I'm looking forward to moving up a bit more now but I still wish I could stay at Lorimer Lane.'

'Put the light on, Jade,' Ruth ordered.

'OK.'

From his chair, Goran emitted a low, complaining groan.

'What have you been doing?' Ruth asked him, holding up the severed cable from the television set.

'Evil things are in there,' he said gruffly.

'Don't be silly, Goran. If you don't want to watch the

25

TV just don't switch it on. There's no need to cut through the flex—especially when it's still plugged in—you could have electrocuted yourself.'

'Evil,' he repeated.

Later, Jade went shopping with her mother. The supermarket was crowded but Ruth seemed not to notice. She selected items at random, tossing them into the trolley without her usual consideration for price and whether they-already-had-these-or-not.

'We don't like sardines, Mum,' Jade pointed out.

'If he's not any better by Monday, I'm calling the doctor,' Ruth replied. 'I should never have shown him that news report.'

'Fine,' Jade smiled, 'but we still don't like sardines!'

Ruth's decision seemed to lift a weight from her shoulders. After piling the food into the car, she took Jade for tea in the nearby Meridian Shopping Centre.

'Why did he do that to the telly?' Jade asked as she coaxed her cucumber back into her sandwich.

'I don't know,' Ruth answered honestly.

'He's not like other people. He's weird,' Jade ventured.

Ruth snapped back instantly. 'Don't say things like that, Jade. If you'd been through half your father's been through you wouldn't say that.'

'What things?' Jade asked.

'Never mind, just don't be rude.'

Rude? Flipping heck, if she wanted to know what rude was she should adopt Navid for a week, then she'd know about it. Stung, Jade focused on her sandwich, not looking up when her mother placed a conciliatory hand on hers.

'Daddy's stressed, that's all. It will pass, then we'll be able to book somewhere for our holidays. Where do you fancy? Ireland again?'

'Not bothered.'

'I wouldn't mind going somewhere hot like Grandma is but we can't shut the shop for that long,' Ruth reflected.

'Ireland's all right,' Jade conceded.

'Mega,' Ruth grinned. 'Now, is there anything you want before we go home?'

Jade glanced across the concourse to Fitzgerald's bookshop. 'Yes. I need a present for Mr Cooper.'

'Does he like sardines?' Ruth asked.

4

School started off fine on Monday for Jade; all her work was finished, she'd given Mrs Gamgee the certificates and Mr Cooper was in one of his daft moods. 'So, the Phantom Letter Nicker has been at it again, Miss Winter. Apparently we have been studying the Ancient *Geeks* all term!' he said, pausing with his staple extractor mid-air.

Jade grinned up at her teacher from the foot of the stepladder as she waited for him to hand her what remained of their history display. 'Could it be the same person who crossed the ''s'' off the scrap paper tray?' she asked mischievously.

Mr Cooper handed her a drawing of Zeus, minus both legs but with the thoughtful addition of a Tippex bra. 'I wouldn't be at all surprised, Watson,' he replied. 'You wouldn't happen to know whether the culprit's name begins with N would you?'

'Might do, might not.'

'If ever a kid pushed his luck, it was that N one, but I'll certainly miss *you* next year,' he said, winking at her.

Jade beamed with pleasure. 'Thanks, sir.'

'That's the trouble with Year Sixes. I just get you well trained and you desert me for secondary school.'

'It's a tough life.'

'You can say that again. Are you nervous about Thursday yet, Miss Outstanding Contributor?'

'A bit,' Jade admitted, stretching to receive two temples and a cardboard amphora. 'Actually, a lot.'

'Oh, don't be—you'll sail through it. Just relax and enjoy yourself. I bet your mum and dad are proud,' Mr Cooper continued.

'Yes,' Jade said quietly, hoping he wouldn't ask further questions.

'I expect your dad's already got the frame worked out for your certificate, hasn't he? What are you having—eighteen carat gold?'

'Do you want me to take the backing paper off?' Jade asked swiftly.

Mr Cooper clanked down from the stepladder, about to say something else when the secretary arrived. Instantly, he dropped to his knees and pretended to beg. 'I'm sorry, Mrs Fell, O Powerful One, but I haven't returned the Leavers' Service reply slips! Be gentle with me on this seriously strenuous Monday afternoon.'

The Powerful One shook her head. 'Don't panic, it's Jade I've come for, though I would appreciate the slips sometime before the service actually takes place,' she said only half-jokingly.

'Just wait one darned second there, girlie!' Mr Cooper protested, brushing the dust from his trousers.

'Can you pop across to Mrs Gamgee's office, Jade? I may be some time,' the fifty-five-year-old 'girlie' smiled.

As she crossed the hall, Jade guessed the summons to see Mrs Gamgee had something to do with preparation for Thursday's service. Maybe she wanted her to escort parents to their seats before the performance? If she did, Jade decided instantly, she would choose Navid and Rosemarie to help her.

She waved at them through the hall window. They were supposed to be painting the stage blocks but seemed to be spraying paint all over themselves instead. Navid grinned and stuck a pair of bright purple thumbs up at her. Laughing, Jade continued towards the Head's room.

Or it could be to do with refreshments, of course. Maybe she'd be asked to pour the orange squash and hand out the biscuits? Unless . . . Jade began to nibble her hair. Unless it had something to do with the certificates.

Less confidently now, she knocked on the office door, entering slowly upon the friendly invitation to 'come in'. Jade's eyes immediately sought out the well-sealed box she had placed on Mrs Gamgee's desk that morning. It had been opened, of course, and the certificates appeared to be perfectly regimented within it. The headteacher followed the girl's gaze and raised her eyebrows. 'Ah, so you know why I've called for you?' she asked.

'Did he get the names mixed up?' Jade guessed tentatively.

Mrs Gamgee peered at her pupil over her half-moon spectacles. 'Jade?'

'Yes, Miss?'

'You did give your dad the certificates to fill in, didn't you?'

'Yes, Miss.'

'Well, he hasn't done any of them, I'm afraid.'

'Not done them?' Jade repeated, feeling her cheeks burn with embarrassment, though the news didn't really surprise her. She might have known, in fact.

Mrs Gamgee feigned a nonchalant shrug, smiling at Jade's pensive face. 'Hey, don't worry, we'll go see if he can do them now, shall we?'

'Now?' Jade swallowed hard. This was a disaster. There was no way on earth she wanted this super-smooth woman to come to the shop which, at any rate, was still closed. Goran had become worse, sleeping all day but awake all night. Pacing the floor, muttering and mumbling, sometimes running up and down the fire escape in the pitch black, as if training for a race. On top of that, he'd started coming out with awful swear words he had never used before and shouting that there were devils everywhere. It was the worst he'd ever been but Ruth was going to make him an appointment for the doctor's as soon as she got to work today. Still, it was vital Mrs Gamgee wasn't allowed anywhere near her home. Not yet, anyway.

Jade stared hard at the box, thinking fast. 'Let me take them on my own, Miss. I know you've got tons to do and Dad's probably in the flat upstairs doing the . . . doing the orders. He doesn't like it if strangers come.'

Mrs Gamgee laughed. 'Hey, I might be strange but I'm not a stranger! Anyway, I need an excuse to pop into Jacob's for a sandwich. I missed lunch again; I'm famished.'

Jade relaxed slightly. She could take the box to her father while Mrs Gamgee was getting something to eat. Knowing Jacob he'd keep Mrs G. talking for ages. She might get away with it. Automatically, she held open the door to allow the headteacher to pass first.

The sun beamed down as the car nosed its way out of Lorimer Lane and in to the heavy traffic of Victoria Street. 'Will your mum be coming to the Leavers' Assembly?' Mrs Gamgee asked casually.

'Yes, if she can get time off from work,' Jade replied.

The headteacher frowned as she was forced to stop behind a line of traffic at the junction between Albert Road and Crimea Street. 'Now what?' she asked. 'There weren't any road works this morning. I hope there hasn't been an accident.'

Glancing briefly at her watch, she indicated right. 'It'll be quicker to walk. I'm going to park outside the Co-op, OK?' Mrs Gamgee pulled decisively out from the stationary queue and slotted immediately into an available space.

Jade's heart began to beat rapidly as the two of them hurried across the street.

At the bottom of Trafalgar Road, the noise increased. Car horns blared impatiently as irate drivers stuck their heads out of windows. In the distance, where the shop was, Jade could see blue police lights flashing in ominous silence. As they neared Inks, Mrs Gamgee slowed, shifting the box from one arm to the other. 'What's going on?' she asked a bystander.

'Some idiot's only parked himself on a table in the middle o't' road.'

'It'll be one o' them Jehovah's Witlesses,' another man added. 'He's going on about evil and all that cobblers.'

'Well, if that's all, can you excuse us? We've got business down here,' Mrs Gamgee said briskly, elbowing her way through. Jade followed reluctantly. She had a sickening feeling about all this.

They were nearer now, squeezing through the densest part of the crowd. 'What's he doing?' a woman asked her husband.

'Chucking stuff.'

'What stuff?'

'Pens by the look of it—from that cabinet he's stood on!'

'Pens?'

'Maybe it's a publicity stunt.'

'No—he's disturbed, poor love. Let's not watch.'

It was then Jade knew her instincts had been right. She craned her neck to see exactly where her father was, to find out what he was doing, but she wasn't tall enough. Mrs Gamgee was. Taking one horrified look at Mr Winter's flailing arms and distorted, wretched face, she bundled her charge through Jacob Krazinski's doorway.

There, Jacob's teenage granddaughter, Rachael, was straining against the window, trying to get a better view. When she saw Jade, her mouth opened then closed again quickly. Mrs Gamgee smiled with relief at her ex-pupil. 'Hello, Rachael. Is your grandfather around?'

Rachael shook her head. 'He's out there, trying to calm Mr Winter down.' The girl turned to Jade, puzzled. 'Have the police sent for you to persuade him to come quietly too, J? Your mum's trying but she isn't doing much good and *Dziadek* should be back in here. He's got a bad heart.'

'My mum's here?' Jade asked worriedly.

Rachael nodded. '*Dziadek* telephoned her when your dad pulled that massive cabinet into the street.' The girl faltered. 'I don't think you should be here, J. Why don't you go back to school?'

Mrs Gamgee nodded her agreement. 'What a good idea. Is there a way out of the back?'

Rachael pointed to a plastic-curtained doorway behind the counter. Mrs Gamgee reached out for Jade's hand but the girl had already slipped through the main door and out into the crowded street. 'Jade! Jade, don't!' Mrs Gamgee called, vainly dashing after her.

Instead of trying to fight her way through the forest of legs, Jade squatted by the far side of the patrol car, hidden from view. An animal instinct had taken over her movements now; the need to be by her mother's side overcoming everything else. Thinking fast, she guessed Ruth would have to pass close by at some stage. As soon as she saw her, she'd run to her, but not before. She had to bide her time.

A loud football cheer suddenly erupted around her. She shrank closer to the wheel of the car and listened. 'The coppers have got him now,' someone sneered. 'Look at him—it's a straitjacket job, is that.'

'Don't be rotten,' another voice protested, 'he can't help it.'

Jade concentrated only on what she saw, not what she heard. Her heart beating rapidly, she waited until the police officers' dark trouser legs came into sight; their polished boots visible on the other side of the car. She saw their feet shuffling as they struggled to keep hold of her writhing, abusive father and open the door at the same time. Roughly, one of them shoved Goran into the rear seat. 'I'll sit with him,' a soft voice stated.

'Are you sure that's wise, love?' an officer asked.

'I want to be with him.'

It was then Jade leapt up, hurling herself round the back of the car, arms outstretched towards her mother. 'Mum! Mum!' she screeched her voice high-pitched and desperate.

Ruth Winter turned, startled at her daughter's unexpected appearance. Her nerves already shredded, the woman leaned rigidly against the side of the vehicle as Jade tried to wind her arms tightly around her waist. Too fraught to return Jade's embrace, Ruth searched the sea of bemused spectators for assistance. Fortunately, Jacob's trusty face swam into view, followed by Mrs Gamgee's.

'You go,' Jacob said firmly. 'I'll look after Jadey.'

'Call my mother—call Sheila,' Ruth directed before turning to Jade. 'I have to help Daddy. Grandma will look after you until I come home. Be good, please.' Her eyes pleaded with Jade who felt as if she was shrinking into the roadside. The baker placed his strong arms around the girl's trembling shoulders, prising her gently but resolutely away from her mother.

Everyone watched as the patrol car began to edge slowly forward, leaving the shocked eleven year old among the bystanders who dispersed like shamefaced bullies in a playground, muttering 'aww' and 'poor kid'.

Jacob led the girl in to his bakery, shaking his head in disbelief. 'What a thing! Always such a quiet man, your father. A quiet foreigner like me—no trouble—and then wha!' The baker clapped his hands together, making them all jump. 'Like Vesuvius!'

Neither Jade nor Mrs Gamgee spoke. Tentatively, Rachael approached her grandfather. '*Dziadek*,' she asked politely, 'can I have my lunch break now?' Her grandfather shrugged his permission for her to leave. Jade stared after the girl, wishing she could slip quietly round the back, too, and disappear.

5

An hour later, Jacob sighed heavily and hung up the receiver yet again. 'She is not at home, your grandma.'

At the kitchen table, Jade sat rigidly opposite Mrs Gamgee, trying desperately to appear normal. 'She's probably buying things for her holiday or she might be at Weight Watchers,' she suggested apologetically.

The baker grunted, unhooked his apron from the back of the kitchen door and fastened it round his robust middle. 'Weight Watchers? Och! Women and their diets. Why did God make sugar then? Or chocolate? To look at? To put in a museum? I don't think so. Huh! Excuse me while I go to my business. Weight Watchers! Trying to bankrupt an old man.' With that, he stomped down to the shop.

Mrs Gamgee smiled reassuringly and Jade smiled back, willing to play along for now but she knew what came next. Not here, but at school, her safe place.

The minute she returned to Lorimer Lane, Mrs Gamgee would tell them everything. Hadn't Jade taken enough empty coffee cups back to the staff room in her time to know what went on? Teachers never closed the door properly—she had overheard things she shouldn't on many occasions. Tonight, she, that Jade Winter in Mr Cooper's, would be main topic. Maybe not in an unkind way but that didn't matter. What mattered was the thought of everyone knowing, especially now, so close to the end of term. Desperately she fought back the urge to cry.

'What time does Grandma usually get home from Weight Watchers?' Mrs Gamgee enquired, trying too hard to make it sound as if it wasn't really important.

Jade fired off an answer which was both over-detailed and over-enthusiastic. 'I don't know. Sometimes she goes for coffee with Marion afterwards. They started at the same time. Marion used to be really, really fat and the doctor said to her: "Mrs Lomas, you'll be dead before you're fifty if you don't lose weight," but she didn't take any notice. Then one day a group of drunk boys started laughing at her in the street and calling her a freak and Balloon Lady in front of her kids. The youngest, Brandy, started crying, so Marion went to Weight Watchers the next day and now she's lost ninety-three pounds. But guess what? She still weighs more than Grandma did when she started. Actually, Grandma's not fat, she just thinks she is.'

Mrs Gamgee stared at the half-devoured plate of buns in the centre of the table. 'It's harder for some than others. My sister hates me because I eat like a horse and never put weight on.'

Jade nodded emphatically, glad to have hit upon this topic—every adult she knew had an opinion on food. 'The worst thing about Grandma dieting is that she's started smoking again. I think smoking's worse than being fat, don't you?'

'Smoking is bad for you,' Mrs Gamgee agreed, careful to cover the cigarettes in her handbag with a packet of tissues as she withdrew her mobile phone. 'I'll just call Mrs Fell again and tell her I'll be later than I thought.'

Jade sat, heart hammering, as the headteacher expertly punched the illuminated digits and waited for her secretary to answer. 'Hi, Pam, it's me—listen, I don't know what time I'll be back but can you ask Andrew to hang on for me? Fine, fine. Did the *Evening Post* call? Well, if they do tell them tomorrow afternoon instead of morning, OK?'

Ask Andrew to wait for me, Jade silently repeated. Andrew was Mr Cooper. Anyone with half a brain knew what that meant. Resentment bubbled in the pit of Jade's stomach. *Just go away, Mrs Gamgee, and leave me alone,* she silently willed her. *If you hadn't insisted on bringing that stupid box you wouldn't have known a thing about my life, and it would have been private, like it always has been.*

'Tell you what I'm going to do,' Mrs Gamgee said as soon as she'd hung up. 'I'm going to start signing these certificates—not yours, of course—then the job's done for tomorrow before the reporter from the *Post* arrives. How about if you read the names out from the achievement list for me and I'll fill them in, OK?'

'OK,' Jade agreed reluctantly.

The headmistress hesitated. 'Everything will be all right, you know. They won't keep Daddy at the police station for long. They'll probably send him to a hospital for a little while and—'

Jade interrupted immediately, knowing she sounded rude but there was no way she was going to be drawn into a conversation about *him*. No way. 'I haven't got my school uniform for the High School yet. Mum says knowing me I'll have grown six inches by September and it'll be no good. We're getting it when we come back from our holidays. We haven't booked anywhere but Grandma's going to Cephalonia on Friday with the people from her Book Circle. She always goes to places where her favourite books are set. If I did that I'd go to Narnia and Camp Jellyjam. Where would you go?'

'Er . . . I don't know, but it's a wonderful idea.'

Jade ploughed on, determined to lead the conversation to safety. 'Grandma was worried about me going to the High after that stuff in the paper about those kids selling drugs but Mum told her most schools had a drug problem now and I'm sensible enough to say no.'

Mrs Gamgee smiled softly. 'Jade,' she said, 'you are the most sensible girl I know.'

It was almost another hour before Sheila Winter arrived in Jacob's kitchen, her dimpled face flushed from the dash across the city. Dressed in bright bermuda shorts and a sleeveless T-shirt which read 'Still Sexy at Sixty', she brought a temporary sense of light relief to the kitchen. Proffering her hand, she introduced herself as 'Trouble's Granny' and thanked Mrs Gamgee for staying. 'I'm sorry I took so long—I've only just heard Jacob and Ruth's messages on my answerphone. I came as soon as I could.'

Mrs Gamgee dismissed her apology with a wave of her hand. 'Don't worry, don't worry. Jade's coping very well, aren't you?' She received an obedient nod and continued awkwardly. 'I'd better be going. Will you tell Mrs Winter I hope everything's OK—she can give me a call at home if I can help in any way?'

'Thank you, I'll tell her,' Sheila smiled.

Mrs Gamgee turned to Jade. 'See you tomorrow, Jade. Don't forget to polish those teeth ready for the camera!'

Jade's deep green eyes darted to her shoes. 'I won't,' she promised.

As soon as Mrs Gamgee had left the room, Sheila gave Jade a warm, comforting embrace. 'You poor love. Are you all right?'

Jade sniffed, wiping her suddenly wet eyes roughly with the palm of her hand, unable to speak. Sheila put her arms around her granddaughter's shoulders and led her towards the landing. 'Come on, Trouble, let's get you to the flat. All these delicious smells are making me nervous.'

'How did you get on at Weight Watchers?' Jade asked gruffly.

'Oh, you don't want to know about things like that,' Sheila said.

'I do,' Jade replied earnestly. Anything to take her mind off the afternoon's events.

'I only lost half a blooming pound. That's after starving myself on cottage cheese all week,' Sheila moaned, closing the kitchen door behind her.

'Half a pound's the same as a packet of lard,' Jade quoted.

'Huh! And I'll put that back on just by being in this place,' Sheila complained as she clattered along the hallway and down towards the shop.

In the bakery, Rachael smiled shyly as she served a customer while Jacob, teeming fresh bagels into a deep basket in the window, told them to hang on a minute and he'd come, too.

'You've done enough, Jacob,' Sheila protested. 'You've your own business to run. We'll manage.'

'What about the shop? Do you want me to lock it up? I have put cabinet round back. It's very broken. Dangerous.'

'I picked most of the pens and stuff up—they're over there,' Rachael added, indicating a pile of assorted biros and pencils next to the till. Among them lay the Waterman, its nib crushed, the lapis-lazuli barrel as splintered as a discarded razor shell on a beach.

'He was throwing them about,' Jade said, noticing the puzzled expression on her grandma's face. The customer looked up out of curiosity. Jade quickly scooped up the pens and hurried out of Krazinski's and straight to Inks, intending to leave them on a shelf and then dash upstairs to change out of her uniform.

Despite the bright sunshine outside, the drawn metal shutters had cast a gloom over the interior of the shop, making it difficult to see. Immediately, something

40

crunched under Jade's foot. Squinting at the floor, she made out several heaps of paperclips scattered randomly round the doorway.

Cautiously, she pushed open the door further and reached for the light switch. 'Come on, love,' Grandma instructed from behind as the bulbs pinged into life.

'Grandma,' Jade began, 'oh, Grandma!'

6

They stared at the wreckage, lost for words. The usually neat and organized interior was a shambles. Reams of paper were incongruously stacked like a totem pole in the centre of the floor, surrounded by smashed ink bottles bleeding into the carpet, more crushed fountain pens, ripped up notebooks, and dozens of pencils snapped in half and strewn everywhere.

Gingerly, they picked their way through the mess and headed for the back door that led to their living area above. Upstairs, Sheila lit a cigarette and stared out of the window. 'Don't say anything, Jade,' she warned. 'I know I'm not supposed to smoke in front of you but I'm a bit shaken.'

'It's all right, Gran. I could do with one, too!' Jade joked.

'I mean, I know he's always been a bit . . . '

'Weird,' Jade furnished.

'I was going to say bad with his nerves—but to do that! There must have been hundreds of pounds worth of stock down there. Hundreds! Your grandad'll be spinning in his grave. That's where the money should have gone!' Sheila said, shooting her agitated head in the direction of Computer Heaven. 'I said that right from the start. You could have been living in one of those executive estate houses now if he'd listened and gone into computers.'

'I know,' Jade agreed. Despite being unsure what an 'executive housing estate' was, it was comforting to hear her grandma's criticisms. They meant she was not alone in her thoughts about her father.

Searching briefly for an ashtray and not finding one, Sheila cupped her hand and flicked ash into it. 'Can you find me an ashtray or something, love?' she asked.

Obediently, she headed towards the kitchen. As she reached the hallway, the phone rang. Hesitantly, Jade answered. 'Hello?' she asked nervously.

'Jade, is that you? It's Mum.'

Jade's stomach churned at the sound of the familiar voice. She pressed the receiver hard against her ear, bringing her mother as close to her as she could. 'Are you OK?' she asked immediately.

'I'm fine. Is Grandma with you?'

'Yes, shall I get her?' Jade asked reluctantly, fighting the urge to keep her mother to herself. She had lost her once today and the memory of that still seared through her heart like a branding iron.

'No, there isn't time. Listen, they're taking your daddy to a hospital in a place called North Bellwood; it's miles away apparently but there aren't any spare beds locally—this flu thing that's going round. I'll call you when I know what's happening but it will probably be after tea-time. Go home with Grandma and take your pyjamas in case you need to sleep over.'

'OK, but I will see you later, won't I?'

'Of course you will.'

'Promise?'

'Promise.'

'I love you.'

'I love you, too, Jade, but I've got to go now.'

Jade was left with a sudden hollow buzzing sound in her ear. Quietly, she replaced the receiver and gave her grandma the news. Sheila nodded briefly—it was what she had been expecting. 'That's good, I need someone to help me decide which bikinis to pack for Greece,' she said cajolingly.

In her bedroom, Jade hastily gathered a few nightclothes and toiletries. She had been slightly reassured by the brief conversation with her mother and now wanted to get to Great Richmond, where her grandma lived, as fast as possible. The sooner she arrived, the sooner her mum would appear and that was all that mattered. Studiously ignoring the *Harry Potter* book she had bought as a leaving present for Mr Cooper, she grabbed her CD Walkman from next to it, and dashed out.

In the street, a grave-looking Jacob pressed a bag of doughnuts into Jade's free hand and told her to make sure she ate them while they were fresh. He remained outside the shop long after the car had disappeared, scanning the roadside for any pens or pencils Rachael might have missed.

Jade spent the rest of the day helping Sheila in the garden, picking gooseberries and blueberries from her many fruit trees. As she tilted one branch after another in her search for ripe berries, her grandma would begin one sentence after another. 'I feel sorry for him but . . .' or 'It's not something I'd wish on anyone, but . . .' There was always an unexplored 'but' just as there was always an unripe, sour berry.

'Mum says he's had a hard life,' Jade said.

'Oh, well, we've all had one of those!' was Sheila's cutting response.

It was late by the time Ruth arrived. As soon as she entered the hallway, Jade flung herself at her, gripping her in a silent embrace.

'Give her a chance to catch her breath, chicken,' rebuked Sheila.

44

'It's all right,' Ruth said, swaying gently from side to side with her daughter wrapped safely in her arms. 'I need this.'

'I'll put the kettle on,' Sheila replied, leaving them alone.

'Are you OK?' Ruth whispered.

Jade nodded, her eyes filling with tears.

'It's not been the best day ever, has it?' Ruth continued in hushed tones, gently stroking Jade's head.

Again, Jade could only shrug in agreement, too overwhelmed to reply.

'Were you all right at Jacob's?'

'Aha.'

'I knew you would be. I'm sorry I had to leave you.'

The tears Jade had been battling with all afternoon came then, pouring out in muffled, deep sobs which made her feel dizzy and sick at the same time.

'I had no choice. You do understand, don't you?' Ruth asked brokenly.

'I know,' Jade mumbled.

'I thought I was seeing things when you jumped out at me. It was all so unreal.'

'I'm sorry.'

'No, no, don't be sorry. It was just one of those dreadful things no one could have foreseen. Don't be sorry. I'm sorry.'

Slowly, Jade felt the pain she had carried around with her from the roadside shrivel like a deflated balloon. Her mother had promised to come back and she had kept her promise. Now, she could forgive her for leaving her.

Later, they all sat down to a meal nobody really wanted. Ruth stared blankly at the salad on her plate, defeated by the ordinariness of the act of eating, after the extraordinariness of the day. 'I never want to go through that again,' she said, moving her iceberg lettuce round and round her plate.

'Eat something, love,' Sheila urged.

Ruth simply dropped her fork and pushed her plate away. 'They were wonderful with him, though,' she continued, her face pale and drawn, 'the police, the doctors—wonderful—really kind and helpful.'

'So they should be.'

'Apart from the first one who arrested him, throwing him about like that. He even threatened to spray him with CS gas on the way, you know,' Ruth informed them, her cheeks flaring an indignant pink.

Jade thought back to the way the police officers had forced her father into the car but she hadn't blamed them at the time—they were only human, after all. Her father had been out of control—wild and frightening. 'What's CS gas?' she asked, her own meal untouched.

Sheila swiftly edged a bowl of pickled baby beetroot towards Ruth. 'Nothing, Jade, nothing. Ruth, I don't think Jade needs *all* the details, you know.'

Ruth glanced apologetically across at her daughter. 'I'm sorry, Jade, it's just that it's all so fresh and raw. You hear the words ''nervous breakdown'' but unless you've actually seen one happen you don't understand the enormity of it. He was just so . . . '

Tears welled in her mother's eyes and Jade stood up to comfort her this time, folding her arms round her shoulders. 'It's OK, Mum, it's OK.'

'And I was going to call the doctors anyway, wasn't I?'

'Yes, you were. You were,' Jade reassured her.

'I should have done it sooner.'

Sheila began piling plates through the serving hatch and patted Ruth gently on her shoulder as she passed.

'Now don't go blaming yourself, Ruth. Like you just said, nobody can predict these things. Is that what they've told you it is, then? A nervous breakdown?'

'Not in so many words but it's obvious, isn't it? He's been what they call "sectioned". They think he'll be in for at least four weeks.'

Jade wanted to ask what 'sectioned' meant—it sounded to her as if her father were to be cut up into segments, but Sheila intervened. 'Four weeks? What about the shop?'

Ruth clicked her tongue at what she saw as the ridiculousness of the question. 'Stuff the shop! It's that place that's caused this whole thing!' Ruth declared.

'Rubbish,' Sheila retorted instantly, flouncing into the kitchen and then sticking her head through the hatchway to retrieve the plates. 'It's what he's done to the shop not what the shop's done to him! You want to see the state of it.'

This was followed by a rattling, thudding sound as Sheila began to load the dishwasher. Jade felt the sudden change in atmosphere caused by her grandma's tactless reply. Ruth stiffened, staring aggressively through the hatch. 'I might have known you'd be like this, Mum. Thanks a lot.' With that, she left the table and began snatching her things from the sideboard. 'Come on, Jade, we're going.'

Obediently, Jade rose, not daring to protest. 'What you'll be telling me next,' Ruth spluttered, angrily yanking on her cardigan, 'is that I should have known what would happen if I married a foreigner. Then you'll go on to how we've frittered away all Dad's insurance money, and finally, that nobody had nervous breakdowns in your day; everyone just got on with it!'

Sheila came back into the room, looking shamefaced. 'I'm sorry, love. You know what I'm like, I speak as I find. Sit down and have a cup of tea.'

The apology did nothing to mollify Ruth, who laughed sharply. 'A cup of tea? How typically British! That'll cure it!'

Her mother returned to the kitchen, flicking on the kettle. 'Well, I've coffee instead, if you want.'

'And doughnuts,' Jade added, touching her mother's hand gently.

Ruth turned, saw the pain in her daughter's eyes and sat down heavily on the settee. She rubbed tiredly at her forehead before looking up. 'What sort of doughnuts?' she asked.

Later, after Ruth and Sheila had finished a lengthy, urgent conversation out of Jade's earshot, Ruth rang the hospital. She was told that Goran was heavily sedated and there'd be little point in visiting the next day. 'It'll give you a chance to sort things out at work,' Sheila advised her crestfallen daughter. 'I'll look after Jade.'

'That's OK, I can pick her up after school,' Ruth said.

'I'm not going to school,' Jade said softly.

'Why?' Ruth asked, puzzled.

'I'm just not.'

Ruth sighed. 'I'm too tired to argue with you, Jade. If you don't want to go tomorrow, don't go. I'll meet you for lunch and we can talk about it then.'

Jade lowered her eyes, half-relieved, half-disappointed by her mother's ready acceptance of her missing school and sabotaging her hundred per cent attendance record, along with everything else.

At bedtime, Jade asked her grandma what a nervous breakdown was. Ruth had already explained that 'sectioning' just meant a doctor's order to keep someone

48

in hospital for treatment, for their own protection, whether the patient wanted to stay or not. It had nothing to do with being cut to pieces. She hadn't really explained what a nervous breakdown was, though. She said it was hard to put into words.

Sheila seemed to be struggling, too, plumping up the pillows on the spare bed with unnecessary force. 'It's no good asking me; I've not had much to do with that sort of thing,' she replied brusquely.

'Are they rare?'

'They are in Yorkshire. We certainly never had them when I was growing up. People just got on with life.'

'Mum said you'd say that,' Jade pointed out.

The pillows were given another bruising shake. 'It's how I feel and I can't pretend otherwise. Can you imagine what state the country would be in if we all went like that? Everyone gets depressed now and again but you control it,' she whispered heatedly, even though Ruth had gone back to the flat and there was no one to over-hear.

'Do you get depressed?'

'Of course, sometimes. I was very depressed when Jack died—he meant the world to me, that man—but I didn't go round wrecking the house, did I?'

'What did you do?' Jade asked, sliding into the cool sheets.

'I had a new kitchen fitted and joined the Book Circle. I kept myself occupied.'

'So if Dad had kept himself occupied he wouldn't have had a nervous breakdown?'

'Exactly,' Sheila said, bending down to kiss her granddaughter goodnight, 'but don't go telling your mum what I've said or she'll fly off the handle again—I don't want her falling out with me. It's not her fault he's weak.'

'I won't say anything,' Jade promised. She knew better than to pass on her grandma's inflammatory comments to her mother and vice-versa. Once, she had repeated Sheila's description of Goran as being 'work-shy' and it had caused a massive row. The scene earlier had been nothing compared to that. They hadn't spoken to each other for weeks and it was only the fact that Jade's birthday had occurred that peace had been made at all. It had been awful, being torn between them.

'Goodnight, then, pet,' Grandma said, closing the door behind her.

'Goodnight, Grandma.'

Although she was tired, it took Jade a long time to fall asleep. Her mind kept going through the events of the day, flitting from one scene to the next. If only, she kept thinking. If only Dad had kept himself occupied he would have signed those certificates. If only he had signed the certificates, Mrs Gamgee wouldn't have come to Trafalgar Road. If only she hadn't come to Trafalgar Road, Jade could have gone to school tomorrow, as usual.

She buried her head in her pillow. She could never face school again. How could she? How could she turn up tomorrow for her photograph-taking? Everybody would just look at the picture and say: 'Wasn't she the one whose dad went do-lally in the street?' And as for the Leavers' Service, how could she attend that now? Stand up in front of the whole school with all those parents staring at her from the audience? All those fathers. 'You'll sail through it,' Mr Cooper had said. Fat chance.

It all boiled down to Goran. He was weak, like Grandma said. She was glad he had been sectioned.

7

Jade awoke late the next morning, confused at first as to where she was until she heard her grandma's voice drifting upstairs. Bleary-eyed, she stood at the door of the kitchen, instantly embarrassed to be greeted, not only by Sheila, but her friend from Weight Watchers, Marion Lomas, as well.

'Hello, sweetheart,' Marion said cheerfully.

'Hello, Mrs Lomas,' Jade replied.

Marion patted the chair next to her at the table, her dimpled bare arm shaking as she did so. Jade took the seat, relaxing. She'd met Mrs Lomas a few times before and always felt comfortable with her.

'What do you want for breakfast, Trouble?' Grandma asked.

'Anything,' Jade answered.

'Anything, she says. Just look at her! I was that skinny once!' Marion exclaimed.

'We all were,' Sheila agreed. 'Boiled egg do?'

'As long as the white's hard.'

'I'm sorry to hear about your dad, sweetheart,' Marion said.

'Thanks,' she said, though she didn't know if 'thanks' was an appropriate answer.

'I was telling your grandma our Rob—he's my eldest—has just bought a row of cottages in Fleetby-on-the-Hill—that's the next village on from North Bellwood. Isn't that a coincidence?'

'Yes.'

Her grandma placed a glass of orange juice in front of Jade. 'Marion reckons Rob would let your mum rent one of the cottages for the summer, if she was interested. He's not renovating them until after he's finished another job in Gisburn.'

'It would save her all that travelling to the hospital and back every day,' Marion explained. 'It's a good seventy miles, all told, and that A1's dodgy at the best of times. Anyway, it's always better to have buildings occupied; they're not as likely to get vandalized then.'

'What do you think, Jade? Do you think your mum would be interested?' Sheila asked.

Jade caught sight of the kitchen clock. Nine-thirty; everyone would be filing into the hall for the final practice of the Leavers' Assembly before the photographer came. 'I don't know,' she shrugged.

But Ruth was thrilled. Her eyes shone when Sheila explained about the cottage. 'That's perfect,' she exclaimed as they huddled awkwardly around the one remaining table in McDonald's, knees bumping as burgers and fries and Cokes were distributed. 'I've been given extended leave from work so we could stay there the whole four weeks Goran's in Bellwood—if he has to stay in that long. How soon can we move in?'

Sheila pinched yet another of Jade's chips she 'shouldn't be having'. 'As soon as you like. I don't know what state it's in, though. It's been rented out for years, so the furniture won't be up to much.'

'Well, it's not Ireland but we don't care, do we, Jadey, as long as we can be near your dad?' Ruth grinned.

'Sure,' Jade replied, happy because her mother was happy. Inside, her feelings were less clear. It would be good to get away from the shop and Trafalgar Road and Lorimer Lane. But, on the other hand, she had been looking forward to life in the flat with just her mother. Fleetby-on-the-Hill didn't sound all that exciting, either. What if there was nothing to do? No park or shops or Jacob's to drop into when she was bored?

'I'll phone Marion and arrange it, then, shall I?' Grandma asked.

'Yes, do,' Ruth urged, 'great.'

'I'll cancel my holiday, as well, then I can come with you.'

Ruth shook her head adamantly. 'Mum, no, there's no need for that!'

Sheila fixed her mouth in a firm line. 'Of course there is. Who's going to look after Jade while you're visiting?'

'She'll come with me, of course.'

The firm line changed into a horrified 'O'. Sheila stooped her head, whispering urgently. 'You can't be serious! You can't let a child go to a place like that!'

Ruth responded levelly: 'Of course I can. The psychiatric ward's attached to the main building just like any other ward in the hospital. Patients use the same facilities as everyone else. There's a pleasant reception area with drinks machines and loos—'

But Sheila wasn't having any of that. 'Are you out of your mind? She could be molested or anything. Sometimes the patients dress up as doctors, you know, in disguise. I read about one woman who thought she was Florence Nightingale and—'

'Don't cancel your holiday, Mum, we'll be fine,' Ruth said, her voice deliberately calm.

Jade proffered what remained of her fries towards her grandma. 'We'll be fine,' she assured her. 'And Navid's taught me where to kick rude men!'

'Well, just don't even *talk* to anyone shifty,' her grandma commanded.

'The same goes for you in Cephalonia,' Ruth retorted.

'Yes, Grandma—especially in that bikini!' Jade added.

8

The rest of the week passed in a blur for Jade. She stayed at her grandma's, living a strange half-life, pretending it was normal to be helping to pack suitcases and watch day time TV during school-time. Ruth tried once or twice to persuade her to return to school but she refused and Ruth didn't pursue it. 'It's easier this way, anyway,' Sheila would add in Jade's defence, 'you can concentrate on sorting yourself out and not have to fret about being back in time for school and cooking meals.'

On Thursday Sheila took Jade to see *The Ghoul's Night Out* at the multiplex cinema on the ring road. The end of the film coincided with the end of the Leavers' Service. 'Well, I'm glad that's over,' Jade sighed as they left the foyer.

Sheila nodded, misunderstanding. 'You and me both. Why they can't just show the original I just don't know— you can't beat Boris Karloff for horror. And don't start me on the price of popcorn! Outrageous!'

After Thursday there was only Friday to get through and that would be that, Jade told herself. That funny feeling of skiving off would disappear and she would be able to relax, wouldn't she?

Friday was hectic because they had to drive Sheila to the airport then go straight on to view the cottage before visiting the hospital afterwards.

It seemed a long journey. The A1 was clogged with heavy traffic and boring stretches of road works every few miles. Once they left the motorway, the quieter roads brought their own problems, with slothful tractors and few signposts to guide them in the right direction.

'It could be Ireland,' Ruth smiled as they drove deeper and deeper into the sun-drenched countryside.

'Could be,' Jade agreed, staring glumly out of the window. *If we weren't on the way to a psychiatric ward.*

It was mid-afternoon by the time they arrived in Fleetby-on-the-Hill but the owner of Church Cottage, Rob Lomas, was already there, grinning warmly at them. 'All reet?' he asked.

'Yes, thank you, and you?' Ruth replied, trying to hide her horror at the condition of the building behind him.

Jade decided straightaway that Church Cottage was haunted. She had read enough ghost stories by now to know the telltale signs, and they were all here. First, there was the overgrown, cracked pathway leading to the dilapidated door with small, dark windows on either side of it. Second, Mr Lomas was having great difficulty in finding the right key—every one he tried made a hollow, grating sound. The ghosts not letting him in, obviously. Most obvious of all, Church Cottage backed onto a graveyard—a dead give-away. 'Blinkin' things,' Rob muttered, trying yet again with another of the long, ancient keys on the ring.

This time, something clicked, and the ruddy-faced builder aided the door along with a fierce kick from his steel-capped boot. 'I'll oil it before I go, Mrs Winter,' he promised. Ruth smiled passively and followed him in. The door opened straight into the single ground floor room that smelt of dry powder paint and thick dusty sheets.

Instantly, every negative thought Jade had felt on the journey over dissolved. She loved it here.

Ruth was less impressed. 'Is this it?' she asked.

Marion's son nodded, grunting as his head hit the low ceiling beam. 'It were only a row o' farm worker's cottages, see, small and simple, no frills. Mind you, by t' time I've finished wi' 'em it'll be "a tasteful conversion in the heart of this much-sought after village" as t'estate agents say.' He frowned for a second, aiming a dirty thumb at the chimney breast. 'So long as I can get hold of the end house. Can't do much without that and the old lass in there won't budge. I've offered her landlord a right fair price, and all. Still, shouldn't have long to wait by the looks of her, if you know what I mean.' He grinned sheepishly and winked at Jade.

'Can I see upstairs?' she asked.

'Aye, up you go.'

Her mother had other ideas. 'Just a minute, Jade, I want to finish in here, first. Where's the kitchen?' she asked.

Rob strode over to a pair of large cupboard doors adjacent to the chimney. He tugged the doors apart to reveal rows of empty shelves above a huge sink and water tank. 'Clever, eh?'

'You must be joking!' Ruth exclaimed. She didn't know whether to laugh or cry.

'That's a Belfast sink, that is,' he continued cheerfully, 'all the rage with trendy townies, they are.'

'What am I meant to cook on?' Ruth continued.

The cupboard beneath the sink area was yanked open. From a dark recess, Rob produced a camping stove. 'I'll get some meths before I go,' he promised again.

'It's a good job my mother's not here,' Ruth laughed, 'she'd have a fit.'

'Can we go up, now?' Jade asked again.

Her mother shook her head ruefully, glanced at the battered sofa and mismatching armchair and waited for Rob to escort them to goodness only knew what.

The stairs were dark and narrow but didn't creak half as much as Jade would have liked. At the top, the landing was too small for the three of them, so Jade waited on the steps until Rob pushed open the door to his left. Rather than following them, she opened the remaining door opposite and investigated by herself.

She entered a large, airy room flooded with sunlight. Her heart danced as she took in the old-fashioned flowery wallpaper, the grey, gypsum floor, the tiny, wrought iron fireplace and the bare window through which light splashed in welcome. The only piece of furniture, apart from a bed, was a large wooden desk pushed against the far wall. Jade gazed at it, longing to explore beneath the roll top which billowed like a fat man's stomach.

'Oh, there you are!' Ruth exclaimed, stepping into the bedroom.

'Look at the desk, Mum,' Jade said.

'It's beautiful; your dad would like that—more than he'd like having to go through the bedroom to get to the bathroom,' she said cynically, referring to the room she had just left.

'It came with the property,' Rob explained, rubbing the desktop with his overall sleeve. 'I'll probably send it for auctioning when I get two minutes.'

'What's inside?' Jade enquired.

'Dunno. Have we to have a look?' Rob asked.

Ruth interrupted, glancing at her watch. 'We haven't time—I want to get to the hospital.'

'We'll be quick, won't we, Jade?'

'Five minutes,' Ruth warned, retreating back downstairs to inspect the 'kitchen' again.

'Let's 'ave a dekko shall we?' Rob said. He slid his hand under the brass lever and heaved. The lid yielded slowly, almost grating into its darkened recess as if it had rheumatism. 'Now then,' Rob said grandly, stepping back to allow Jade to see.

Inside was disappointingly empty. There was an ordinary wide and dusty surface on which to write but at the back four rows of tiny drawers, each with a glass knob the size of a ten pence piece, made up for the otherwise plain content. 'Oh, aren't they lovely!' Jade cried, already planning what she would use them for.

Rob reached forward, pulling first one then another of the drawers out. 'No treasure,' he laughed, showing her the ink-stained contents. 'Back to the lottery!'

'I don't care there's no treasure. Please may I use the desk while I'm here?' Jade enquired.

'Seeing as you've asked so nicely,' the builder nodded.

Jade ran downstairs. 'When can we move in, Mum?' she cried excitedly. Even if Church Cottage wasn't haunted, it was perfect in every other way. She frowned when she saw the hesitation in her mother's eyes, sensed her reluctance to take on the cottage. 'You said it didn't matter what state it was in. You said!' Jade reminded her.

'Look,' Rob interrupted, 'if you clean the place up a bit, you can have it rent free. That way at least I know it's occupied while I'm working away. How's that sound?'

'Well, if it wasn't for the fact that it's so close to the hospital I'd not touch it with a bargepole, Rob, I'm sorry,' Ruth said begrudgingly.

'Mum, please!' Jade begged.

Ruth gazed at Jade's bright face, recognizing it was the first time she had seen her so animated in days. 'OK, seeing as my daughter seems so struck on the hovel, I'll take it, as long as you remember who's doing who the favour here!'

'Yes!' Jade cried triumphantly. 'We'll move in tomorrow, first thing,' she told Rob.

'Very well, boss,' the builder laughed.

9

After saying goodbye to Rob, they headed for the hospital. Bellwood was five miles from Fleetby-on-the-Hill, taking them only ten minutes to reach by car. Jade had expected it to be deep in the countryside, away from houses and people, but it was on the outskirts of North Bellwood, a large market town.

'Do I have to come in?' Jade asked as her mother pulled into the visitor's car park and sought a parking spot.

'What do you mean?'

'Can't I just wait in the car? I'll keep the doors locked.'

Ruth frowned, concentrating on reversing between two badly parked vehicles. 'What's she been saying?'

'Who?' Jade asked innocently.

'You know who. Mrs Unsympathetic of Great Richmond, that's who.'

'Nothing.' Nothing she could tell her mother about, anyway. Before leaving for Cephalonia, Grandma had given her strict instructions not to talk to anyone in the hospital, not to sit on the toilet seat, and not to leave Ruth's side for one second. She had also advised Jade not to mention her father was on a psychiatric ward to anyone she met at Fleetby. 'It doesn't do to be as open as your mother, pet,' she had warned. 'People are still funny about this sort of thing—best to say he's working abroad or whatever.'

Ruth guessed some 'pearls of wisdom' had been passed on. 'Look, Jade, this is your father we're talking about.

He needs us now, more than ever. We're all he's got, you know.'

'I know.'

'Well then.'

'It's just . . . '

Ruth pulled on the handbrake and switched off the engine. 'It's "just" nothing. Now come on—you can choose something from the shop to take up to the ward. What do you think he'd like? Sweets? A magazine?'

Jade stared at the rubber matting of the car's floor, chewing hard on her hair. Why couldn't her mother see she didn't want to choose anything for *him*, not because of what her grandma had said, but because she was scared? Scared he'd be muttering swear words or throwing his arms around or letting spit dribble on to his chin—in front of the whole hospital. How could she choose sweets for someone like that?

Ruth ruffled Jade's hair, gently easing the wetted strands out of her daughter's mouth. 'You have a think about it while I get the ticket.'

The reception area was as pleasant as her mother had described. Freshly painted in duck-egg-blue emulsion with a wide flowery border snaking all the way round the lobby and up the stairs, it felt reassuringly like a doctor's waiting room.

Jade began to relax a little as she followed her mother to the reception desk. She hung back slightly, as the smartly dressed receptionist slid the protective window open and greeted Ruth with a smile.

Ruth leaned forward. 'I've come to see my husband, Goran Winter, on Trent Ward? I wasn't sure whether we could go straight up or not; it's the first time he's been awake enough to see us.'

The receptionist, Janet Spivey, according to her name badge, quickly skimmed a roster in front of her. 'If you go to the desk on the ward before you see your husband, Mrs Winter, they'll be able to bring you up to date,' she informed her, then glanced at Jade. 'How old is your little girl?' she asked.

'Eleven.'

'I'm sorry, we don't recommend anyone under the age of thirteen on the wards, just as a precaution.'

'Why not?' Ruth asked, puzzled. 'Goran's in his own room, he's not with other patients.'

The woman rubbed away a hard speck on the face of her watch before replying patiently: 'That was only until the acute episode had passed, he's on the main ward with everyone else now. I'm sorry, it's hospital practice. When he's feeling better, Mr Winter can come down into reception here and sit with you during visiting—or there's the Day Room.'

'But what can I do today? We've travelled miles.'

'I'm sorry, I know it must be awkward.'

Ruth's shoulders sagged in disappointment. 'I should have checked, I suppose, but I just presumed she'd be allowed up.'

'Look,' Janet offered, 'I'll get someone to cover the desk and I'll sit with . . . what's your daughter's name?'

'Jade.'

'I'll sit with Jade.'

Ruth turned, her face anxious and drawn, remembering the last time she had left her. 'What do you think, Jade? Will you be all right with that?'

'Yes, no problem,' Jade assured her brightly. Secretly, she was relieved to have wriggled out of seeing her father so easily.

The arrangements were made and Jade waved goodbye as her mother rounded the corner and headed for Trent

Ward, promising she wouldn't be long. Janet led Jade towards the drink machine in the corner of the waiting room. 'What do you fancy?' she asked. 'I'm going for Diet Lilt.'

Jade declined the offer. 'So,' Janet continued, trying to make small talk with her unexpected charge. 'Have you broken up from school already? They don't finish until today round here.'

'Erm . . . we don't either, but it was just tidying up and stuff so Mum said it didn't matter,' Jade replied in a quiet voice. She glanced at the clock above a framed picture of boats at sea. Four-thirty. It was totally over now, anyway. She had left Lorimer Lane School forever with nothing to show for it. No certificate. No trophy. No final 'thumbs up' from Mr Cooper, whose present was gathering dust on her dressing table. Nothing. A hollow feeling in the pit of her stomach arrived out of nowhere. It seemed to fill her insides with stale air. 'I think I will have a drink,' Jade said.

Janet smiled kindly, handing the pale-faced child the coins so she could choose for herself. As Jade fed the money into the slot, a girl suddenly flounced into the waiting room and leaned heavily against the dispenser. 'Bloody cow!' she said.

Jade stared at her in surprise, dropping a twenty pence piece. The girl automatically stretched out a white skinny leg and stamped on the coin with a heavy boot.

'Here,' she said, handing the coin back to Jade, 'don't have the Coke; it's foul.'

'Thanks,' Jade said, selecting an orange soda.

'What's wrong, Molly?' Janet asked.

'Won't see me, will she? Says I'm better off without her and to forget she exists. Self-pitying old cow!'

'Give her a chance, Molly. It was very close this time.'

'You don't have to tell me—I found her!' the girl

63

exclaimed. 'Can you lend me fifty p.?' she asked Jade abruptly.

Jade shook her head, trying not to stare at Molly, whose dramatic bleached hair frizzed out at all angles like white candy floss. It was hard to tell her age: from her voice, she could have been about twelve or thirteen, but from her make-up—electric blue eye shadow, thick black eyeliner, and gold nose-stud, she looked a lot older—maybe fifteen or sixteen.

'Sorry,' Jade said, 'I haven't got any money.'

The girl turned to the receptionist. 'What about you, Miss Spivey? Will you buy me a drink? I'm gagging. It's baking in here.'

The obliging Miss Spivey delved into her pocket for yet more change.

'Cheers,' Molly smiled, punching the machine's keypad expertly. 'So,' she said, returning to Jade as soon as she had taken a deep slurp from her can, 'who's the nutter in your family? Mine's me mam. She's going for the *Guinness Book of Records* in stomach pumping.'

'Molly,' Janet interrupted sternly.

'What?'

'Not everyone's as forward as you are.'

Molly snorted. 'Listen, Miss Spivey, it's nothing to do with being forward. It's about not pretending, isn't it? But only people like you, what works here, and people like us . . . ' Here, the girl waved a nibbled finger back and forth between herself and Jade, 'what's been on the receiving end, understands, isn't that right, kid? I presume you're visiting a fruit and nut cake, like me?'

Jade flinched but nodded anyway, which was all the encouragement Molly needed. She launched into a non-stop talk about her mother's numerous suicide attempts. Although each story was appalling, Molly re-told it so blithely Jade ended up giggling loudly at most of the descriptions. 'And I said to her, Mam, at least wear knickers next time you try to top yourself!' Molly finished.

'Molly!' Janet admonished several times but neither girl listened.

'So, which one of your 'rents is it?' Molly asked, offering Jade a piece of Hubba-bubba.

'My dad.'

'What is he? Manic? Schizo? Junkie? Alky? I've seen 'em all, you know. Related to most of 'em.'

Normally, Jade would not have replied but Molly was different. As funny and flippant as Navid, but better, because she knew how it felt to have a parent who wasn't like other parents. Forgetting her grandma's advice she said, 'He's had a nervous breakdown—he went berserk in the street and got arrested.'

Molly nodded ferociously. 'Huh! Mental people are the worst to live with, aren't they? That's cos they're mental!' Several heads turned to stare and Janet grimaced but Molly continued unabashed. 'One minute they're high as Heaven, laughing and singing and expecting you to join in, then they're rock bottom and so, so snoring-boring; it's curtains drawn and *turn that racket down* and *leave me alone* and *oh, why me*? And we have to put up with it, don't we? We have to get up and go to school and hand in our homework on rainforests, as if nothing happened the night before, apart from *Coronation Street*.'

Or miss important events altogether, Jade thought as the girl continued her tirade, barely stopping for breath.

'We have to put up with the other kids' sarky comments and nudge-nudges from them watching behind their net curtains when the ambulance turns up again. Nobody's crowding round our bed, bringing us chocolates and making a fuss and telling us they understand what it must be like, what with the bills to pay and the pressure of bringing up the children on your own. Huh! It's us that should be getting the choccies and the fuss—the—what's your name?'

'Jade Winter.'

'The Jade Winters and the Molly Hepworths of this world.'

Jade felt dazed. Molly had put into words precisely what she felt. 'Still,' Molly added, 'they're all we've got and nobody's perfect, are they?'

'No,' Jade agreed.

'Though I come damn near, sometimes. Do you think I've got nice legs, kid?' Molly stood up, posed like a malnourished ballerina on tiptoes.

The 'kid' grinned. She sensed an empathy with this brash girl that she had never felt with any of her school friends. Molly grinned back in silent acknowledgement and drained the remains of her can. She burped, then tossed it in the bin. Jade laughed and was about to ask Molly more questions when the older girl suddenly grabbed hold of Miss Spivey's wrist and shrieked. 'Bloody Norah! I'll miss me bus! See you!' She headed for the exit, yelling over her shoulder, 'We'll go to the Day Room next time—there's a telly in there.'

'OK,' Jade agreed.

'Cheers, then, Jade. See you, Miss Spivey.'

The girl dashed out, her boots squelching on the shiny floor.

'She's a case, that one,' the receptionist said fondly. 'She's seen worse things in her life than any fourteen year old deserves to have seen, yet she bounces back every time.'

Of course she does, Jade thought, *she has to*.

'Lousy bureaucracy' was the main topic on the journey home. 'I still think it's ridiculous you can't go on the ward. I felt dreadful leaving you alone down there. And after me convincing your grandma there wouldn't be any problems,' Ruth blazed. 'It's a good job she's on the other side of the Mediterranean or I'd never hear the end of it. What are people supposed to do? What about single parents? Or those who can't afford childcare?'

She paused to overtake a Tesco lorry before pulling back into the inside lane. A scrunched up cigarette packet was tossed from the van in front of them. 'Litter lout!' Ruth yelled. 'And stop doing that, for goodness' sake,' she snapped at Jade, who had begun to chew her hair. 'If you're hungry we'll stop off at the next Little Chef.'

'Fine by me,' Jade replied, hurt by the irritation in her mother's voice.

'I'm sorry,' Ruth said instantly, 'I'm just a bit upset. The doctor thinks it would be best if I didn't visit for a couple of days to give him a chance to work things through with Dad. I wish I hadn't taken the cottage on, now. It's a waste of time. I could have just paid Rachael to babysit for you and put up with the travelling when at least we'd have had our home comforts instead of living in that dump. It just seems to be one problem after the other. In fact, I'm going to call Rob as soon as we get in and cancel everything. He's got a nerve anyway; it's virtually uninhabitable, that place.'

Jade began to panic. She couldn't lose the cottage and Molly so soon. 'There's a café ahead, Mum, let's stop there,' she suggested. 'We can have a coffee then and talk things through.'

'You sound like a therapist now!' Ruth complained but she slowed and pulled onto the slip road leading to the Dixie Diner.

Jade waited until the waitress had taken their order before pouncing. 'Don't cancel the cottage, Mum, please. It'll be ace once we've tidied it up and it's so convenient for Bellwood and it's like . . . ' She paused, searching for the clincher, 'it's like that cottage we saw in Ireland last year that Dad liked. He said he'd love to live there, in the middle of nowhere, didn't he?'

Ruth frowned, trying to remember. 'It's nothing like it! The Irish cottage was pink for a start, with a thatched roof and an orchard.'

'Well, it's nearer to it than Trafalgar Road is! If Dad gets better quick he can come and live in Church Cottage with us instead of going straight back to the flat, can't he?'

'Well, I hadn't thought that far ahead,' Ruth said, smiling wanly as the waitress set down their order of milky coffee and ice-cold Coke. She sighed heavily. 'Dad was still lethargic. He could hardly speak, they've got him so full of sedatives.'

Jade didn't reply. She wanted to talk about the cottage and Molly, not him, but her mother continued, her voice distant, as if trying to fathom something out. 'The doctors don't seem to think his breakdown was caused by stress from the shop—that was just the final straw. And all the other stuff, the swearing and the running up and down and everything were just *symptoms*.'

So Grandma had been right, Jade thought, the shop wasn't to blame.

'If only I'd been more aware, I could have made him see someone sooner—I was just hoping the bad patch would pass, like it usually does,' Ruth said miserably, repeating what she had said at Sheila's. Jade stared stolidly at the floor, wanting to reassure her mother it wasn't her fault Goran was weak but she knew Ruth would be angry if she dared make such a suggestion. Instead, she listened as her mother continued. 'They feel—well, Doctor Michaels that I spoke to feels—that all this has more to do with the past and his family. Goran's talking about his mother a lot.'

'Why?' Jade asked. Unlike with her Grandad Jack, there were no photographs in silver frames, ornaments won at seasides, or rosettes for best kept allotments, as mementos of a past life. Grandma Alma was a name and nothing else.

Ruth sipped slowly from her cup. 'It could be one of a million things; Daddy's got such a muddled background. I'm sure I don't know half of it. I told Dr Michaels he always clams up, doesn't he, if we bring his mother into the conversation?'

'You both do,' Jade stated.

'What do you mean?' Ruth asked testily.

Jade hesitated. She hadn't meant that to come out the way it sounded. 'Nothing,' she said quickly.

'No, it's important—I can tell it is,' Ruth said. Her eyes softened. 'I won't bite, you know!'

'OK,' Jade said. 'Do you remember when I was trying to trace our family history for that school project, and Dad wouldn't even give me names or places or anything about his side? And all I found out was I should be called Jade Andvijevica by rights because when you got married Dad took your name instead of keeping his?'

'Yes.'

'And I got fed up because I'd drawn a huge tree on sugar paper and I could only fill in half the branches and you told me off for being stroppy.'

'Did I?'

'Yes, you did. I asked you to find out for me and you said not to push it because he didn't want reminders.'

'Well, it was true, he didn't. Besides, you drew those fantastic rosy apples on the tree and got a merit award anyway, didn't you?'

Jade faltered. Ruth couldn't understand how that was beside the point; how it had seemed like another example of her father's indifference to her. Another ordinary request rejected to add to all the others. 'Everyone thought you were divorced,' she explained feebly.

'I'm sorry,' Ruth said, though it was clear to Jade she didn't really know what she was apologizing for.

'It doesn't matter. Shall we go now?'

Ruth took another sip from her coffee. 'You're right, you know.'

'About what?'

'The cottage. Dad might be out quite quickly and it would be nice for him to recuperate somewhere other than Inks. And the village looked nice . . .

' "Much sought after",' Jade quoted.

'Go on, then, Dump Cottage it is!' Ruth grinned.

'Yes!' Jade yelped loudly, making all the customers' heads momentarily turn towards their table.

'You'll have to wear slippers all the time so you don't get splinters in your feet,' Ruth warned.

'Fine.'

'There's no Sky TV.'

'Not bothered.'

'You'll have to come through my bedroom to get to the bathroom.'

'Not bothered.'

'There's no telephone to call your mates and it's too expensive to use my mobile all the time.'

'Not bothered.'

'You'll have to wash up, too, and share with the meals—I'm on holiday as well.'

'Like I don't do that already!'

'You won't be dissuaded, will you?' Ruth grinned.

'Not in a million years,' Jade grinned back.

The journey home was so much better than the one coming. They had the radio on full-blast, singing along to the music, heads jigging from side to side, voices getting louder and louder with each drumbeat. 'Can I invite Molly over one day?' Jade asked during the commercials.

'The girl you met in Bellwood? Sure.'

'Thanks.'

'Rosie and Navid could sleep over, too, I suppose, if we fetched them.'

Jade shook her head. Rosie and Navid belonged to another time, another place. 'No thanks, just Molly,' Jade replied.

'Just Molly,' Ruth repeated.

10

Early next morning, the ever-helpful Rob turned up to load his transit van with small bits of furniture and other useful paraphernalia for Church Cottage. 'I've already oiled the lock and bought the meths as promised, Mrs Winter,' he announced.

Jade's mother smiled blearily before piling the rest of what they'd need for the four weeks or so into her car, including the meths-free microwave. She then proceeded to double-check Inks was locked properly and adjusted the 'Closed until further notice' sign while Jade huddled in the back, snuggling down in her sleeping bag. 'All set,' Ruth said. 'Those people did a good job,' she added, referring to the firm of cleaners contracted to tidy the shop after the devastation.

Jade waved to Jacob, who was dressed in his dark suit, ready for the synagogue. He had promised to visit soon, as well as to forward any post that arrived. Not that there'll be any, apart from bills and junk mail, she guessed. Neither Mrs Gamgee nor Mr Cooper had left a message on the answerphone, as she had half hoped they would. Well, they could get lost, for all she cared. Lorimer Lane was history. What was it that Thomas kid had said about secondary school? It was a fresh start? Well, she was having her fresh start now, away from the whole bunch of them. As the engine spluttered into life, Jade snuggled down further, closed her eyes, and went back to sleep.

*　*　*

It took the pair of them the whole day to clean the rooms. 'I think I'd rather have paid rent and let Rob sort this out,' Ruth said, blowing a damp strand of hair from her face.

'But it looks fantastic, Mum,' Jade said. She'd had a wonderful morning, attacking cobwebs, beating carpets and scouring the Belfast sink. The front room glowed, especially with the addition of their Chinese rug in front of the fireplace and candles on the deep windowsill. Upstairs, Jade had laid out her sleeping bag on top of the mattress, swept her bedroom floor, and polished the outside of the desk with Mr Muscle.

Then she had filled the tiny drawers with her writing and drawing things—sharpeners, erasers, rubber bands in one set; felt pens, pencils, cartridges in the other. For the desk itself, her mother had brought her a writer's blotting pad from Inks, to prevent any marks and scratches to the wood. The lapis-lazuli pen would have been perfect for the desk but Jade blocked out that thought as soon as it occurred to her. The one she had would do. Happy with her display, she ran downstairs, taking the steps two at a time.

The plan had been to go out for an evening meal in the village pub, The Black Bull, but instead they settled on a makeshift picnic downstairs. Ruth left the door open, so that the warmth and sunshine could join them. 'It's great here, isn't it?' Jade said.

Ruth smiled. 'You've really taken a shine to the place, haven't you?' She glanced round, staring at the mottled brown tiles of the boarded-up fireplace. 'I guess it's not *that* bad, now that it's cleaned up a bit. Maybe we should go for a walk tomorrow; find out a bit more about the village?'

'OK.'

'There would have been a lead range there once,' Ruth said, indicating a ridge of rough plastering midway up the

73

chimney breast. 'The poor wife would have baked bread in it and boiled water on it and hung clothes above it and kept the fire going on top of it all.'

'Daft place to have a fire—on top of it all, specially near the washing,' Jade teased.

'You know what I mean, Miss Pedantic. Then when her husband had finished in the fields he'd sluice himself down in the yard before coming in and demanding his dinner.'

'Where's me grub, wife!' Jade improvised in a gruff voice.

Ruth laughed and began clearing away the food things. 'Thank goodness your dad was never like that,' she said.

Jade rose to help her, stacking the plates and beakers on the draining board. 'I think Rob should leave the cottages as they are, just repair them. Then three families can live here instead of one posh one.'

But Ruth didn't reply. She had that far-away expression on her face and Jade knew her thoughts were with Goran in Bellwood, not her.

Upstairs, Jade sat with her knees tucked under her chin, her back pressed against the flowery wallpaper, gazing out of her bedroom window. She could almost feel the decades of history seep through her T-shirt and into her skin, as if the cottage were claiming her as one of its own. It wasn't ghosts the cottage had, she realized, just a sense of things past.

The window was so low, almost to floor-level, she had no trouble seeing out into the graveyard below. St Cecilia's Churchyard was not very large, perhaps half the size of a school playground. The grass was overgrown and wild, splattered with yellow dots of dandelions and buttercups, cow parsley and dock leaves. The majority of the graves were sandstone; weathered and lichen crusted. Many were leaning sideways after years of fighting the elements. One particular grave, larger than the others, with a fancy barley-sugar twist rail surround and triangular marble tomb, appeared to be sinking into a grassy sea. None of the graves had fresh flowers; a fact which pleased Jade. It meant few people came, and she could pretend the place was her garden.

A woman pushing a pram had entered from the side gate to Jade's left, shattering that idea. The woman's face wasn't clear but Jade knew she was old. Every manoeuvre suggested age: the hunched way she held her shoulders, the slow, dragging walk as if each step were painful to take, and the tight grip on the pram handle with hands too knobbled to unbend.

The woman's clothes were really odd, Jade thought, not just out of date but properly old fashioned, like Mary Poppins gone wrong. She had stopped in front of the large grave, the one with the fancy surround. For a while, she just stood there, staring silently at the grave. *As silent as the grave*, Jade smiled to herself. Then the old biddy began to talk, working her shrivelled mouth up and down with words Jade could not hear but could feel. They were angry, venomous words. Jade shrank back, fearful that she should be seen.

A strand of white hair fell across the woman's face and she pushed it away, becoming more and more agitated. She was moving now, along the foot of the grave, stepping backwards and forwards, backwards and forwards, almost agile in comparison to her slow arrival. Time and time again she pointed to the pram, then jabbed the same finger at the gravestone. Suddenly, she leaned her head back and spat fully onto the grave's marble roof.

Jade had seen enough. Cautiously, she withdrew from the window and went to sit downstairs with her mother.

'Everything OK?' Ruth asked, smiling briefly at her daughter before returning to her book.

'Yep,' Jade replied, folding her arms to stop her hands from shaking.

11

I t was cooler the next day, with clouds blowing across the sky. Good walking weather, according to Ruth. They set off after breakfast, heading down the back lane, past the empty middle cottage and the neglected end one. 'Didn't Rob say that was the one the old lady lived in—the one who wouldn't sell?' Ruth asked, staring openly at the bare windows and decaying front door with its broken glass panels.

'I think so.'

'It looks as if she could do with some help with the place.'

Jade glanced briefly at the end cottage, catching sight of a pram handle through the grimy window. So that's where the old woman lived—she might have guessed. Jade felt resentment flood through her. The old woman was another—she groped for a word and settled for Molly's 'nutter'—another *nutter*. Cutting through TV wires, spitting on graves, what was the difference?

Mad people were like road works, Jade thought, every time you thought you'd got through one lot, along came another stretch to stop you in your tracks. Depressed by her thoughts she ran ahead, clambering over a wooden stile and jumping down into the awaiting, spacious field. 'Someone's had their Weetabix,' Ruth called, striding to catch up.

Jade didn't reply.

The field led to acres of pasture and finally to a river, a few murky metres wide. They followed its slumbering, indifferent course for a while before seeing a Private, Keep Out warning and turning back. 'Coffee time,' Ruth declared.

Jade was assigned shop duty for biscuits and *The Sunday Times*. 'Get something really chocolatey,' Ruth instructed. They had already discovered Fleetby-on-the-Hill only had one shop, a grocery-cum-post office run by a curt dark-haired woman called Mrs Lunn.

Gloomily, Jade sauntered along Main Street, barely glancing at the graveyard on the way past. She had no desire to explore it now. That mad pram woman had ruined it for her, breaking the spell with her shouting and spitting. They might as well go back to Trafalgar Road, like Ruth had wanted.

A girl was coming out of the store, carrying two large plastic bottles of Seven Up, as Jade entered. She was slightly shorter than Jade, with a plump, suntanned face and fine, red hair. 'Hi,' she greeted as Jade moved to allow her to pass.

'Hi,' Jade replied.

She realized it was the first time in days she had seen anyone her own age. The last time had been Navid and Rosemarie painting the stage blocks. Determinedly, she pushed open the door and entered the shop, quickly choosing the biscuits and paper. 'You're thirteen pence short,' Mrs Lunn pronounced as Jade handed over the money.

'Sorry,' Jade apologized, digging into her jeans for a twenty p. piece.

Wordlessly, Mrs Lunn slid the change across the counter, allowing Jade to escape.

At the cottage, Ruth pointed to a pile of freshly made sandwiches in the centre of the table. Next to them was an assortment of biscuits and crisps, arranged in cereal bowls. 'Not much of a Sunday dinner but I don't feel like cooking, to be honest,' Ruth apologized.

'I like this better,' Jade replied. Mother and daughter sat opposite each other, cross-legged, sandwiches in one hand, papers in the other. Slowly, Jade found herself unwinding; she dismissed the old woman from her mind and allowed herself to become engrossed in reading and eating. She snuggled deeper and deeper into the prickly chair, outlasting even Ruth's powers of news absorption. Eventually, Ruth laid down *The Sunday Times*. 'Isn't this nice?' She yawned. 'So relaxing.'

'Yes, it's much better without Dad,' Jade said, without thinking. She looked up with apologetic eyes. 'I mean . . .'

'I know what you mean,' Ruth said quietly. 'He isn't the easiest of men to live with.'

Jade waited for her mother to continue, amazed at both the lack of a reprimand and the revelation. 'Shall we talk about it?' Ruth asked.

Jade was about to shake her head but her mother seemed so prepared, so earnest, she agreed. 'I phoned the hospital when you were at the shop,' Ruth continued. 'They said Dad's making wonderful progress. I know it sounds stupid but I think the breakdown's probably the best thing that could have happened.'

To Jade, this seemed a ridiculous thing to say. 'How?' she asked incredulously.

'Because it's released all the things that have been haunting him over the years, since his childhood. He's never been able to talk about them before; he's just bottled them up. It's made me realize how little I know about him, and I'm his wife. It's silly, really, because he can bore for Britain on other things—you know what he's like when he gets fixated on a subject—he never lets up.

Anything to do with things closer to home, though, and that's a different ball game . . . Anyway, then I realized that if I hardly know anything, you know even less about him and that's wrong.'

'Yeah, well,' Jade mumbled.

'What you said in the diner the other day was true. I've been as guilty of hiding things from you as Goran has. I just didn't think little girls should have to know about such things.'

'*Little girls* shouldn't but I should!' Jade said indignantly. 'Why is it that grown-ups think we're babies until we start secondary school? Have they ever listened to Year Sixes in the playground? They swear worse than disc jockeys, you know.'

'OK. Keep your wig on, granny. Who told you to grow up so quick?'

'Bart Simpson,' Jade retorted.

Ruth grinned. 'I've forgotten what I was going to say now,' she grumbled.

'You were telling me that Dad wasn't the easiest person to live with,' Jade prompted.

Immediately, the solemnity returned to her mother's face. 'I think we all need to be open about this mental illness Goran has; we're all part of the same family.'

Jade wriggled in her chair, pulling a strand of hair towards her mouth. For once, Ruth didn't chide her, as she concentrated on her explanation. 'He had so much talent when I met him—he wouldn't have been given a scholarship to come to England to study art otherwise, you know. I fell for him the minute he walked into the bursar's office enquiring about his grant. We'd been advised not to date students but Goran was so different. Vulnerable, I suppose. After a few weeks with him I was head over heels.'

'This isn't going to get sloppy, is it?' Jade teased lightly.

80

Ruth sighed. 'I suppose there were warning signs, even then, but love is blind.'

'So he's always been weird, then?' Jade asked.

'Damaged,' Ruth corrected.

'Damaged?' Jade frowned. She thought of parcels being damaged but not people.

'Yes. It's the word they used at the hospital and I think it describes your dad perfectly. When dreadful things happen to you as a child, it affects the type of person you grow up into.'

'How?'

Jade waited, expecting to be fobbed off with the usual, limp 'never mind' ending. Ruth seemed to sense her thoughts and paused for a second, then plunged on with her answer. 'Well, for example, Goran's father left him when he was four; no reason, just upped and left. I don't care what people say about children being resilient, when something like that happens it's bound to leave some mark on the child.'

Jade thought about Rosie and Navid, who only saw their father every other weekend and how upset it made them if he didn't turn up for his access visit. Navid was always worse on those Mondays, argumentative and troublesome. Jade could see that what her mother said made sense.

'Later Alma re-married someone Goran hated; a real bully who used to take the belt to him for no reason at all. Once he beat Goran unconscious.'

'That's awful!'

Ruth nodded sadly. 'You know, there's always a reason for why people act and behave the way they do, Jade. You have to look for the reason then you can understand the behaviour.'

'I suppose so,' Jade said thoughtfully.

'Poor Goran.'

'What about Grandma Alma? Why didn't she stop her husband from being cruel? You would.'

Ruth picked sorrowfully at a loose thread on her chair arm. 'I don't know. That's another part of the problem. As soon as he was old enough, Daddy left home, only visiting Alma when he knew his stepfather was out. When he won the scholarship to come to England, he went to say goodbye to her but his stepfather was there and wouldn't let him in. He never saw her again.'

'Why didn't he phone or write?' Jade asked.

'Because terrible things were happening in Daddy's country. It was called Yugoslavia then, but when he was a student a war broke out and the part he lived in is now called Bosnia.'

'I know that. He always turns the telly up loud when it's mentioned on the news, before he wrecked it, that is.'

Ruth scratched her chin, wondering how much more to reveal. 'Cutting through the flex was his way of dealing with things he didn't want to hear. No TV, no bad news.'

'One of those symptoms?'

Ruth nodded sadly. 'Exactly. I think with the Kosovo crisis now, it's brought everything flooding back. He came to England in 1986, just before things got really bad the first time. Now, it's flared up again, with all these atrocities. Kosovo is very near to Bosnia, you know? It was bound to remind him of Alma. I think . . . I think she must have been killed but I can't be sure—Goran's never been back to find out the true story.'

Jade felt a surge of pity for her father. If she could have, she would have gone up to that rotten stepfather and kicked him where it hurt.

Ruth ploughed on, comforted by Jade's intense concentration. She had been worried by her daughter's reluctance to talk about her father but she saw now all she needed to do was be straight with her. 'Your gran could never see the attraction, of course. She thought I was throwing my life away marrying an artist—and a foreign one at that. He tried so hard to please her in the early days after my dad died—he even did a course in calligraphy to have a skill he could market. Not that she was any more impressed, of course,' Ruth added bitterly.

'She is always going on about how he should have gone into computers,' Jade admitted.

Ruth nodded. 'Grandma wanted an executive son-in-law to brag about to the neighbours; she got Goran. Serves her right for putting all her eggs in one basket and only having one child.'

'I'm an only child,' Jade pointed out.

'Ah, but you were different. Your grandma only wanted one child because she was frightened of losing her figure. I wanted four or five children, at least, but your dad didn't want any.'

'I didn't know that.'

'It's not something you tend to discuss!'

'So he didn't want me?' Jade said, hurt.

Her mother hesitated. 'No, he didn't want *children*. He thought it was irresponsible bringing new life into such a crazy world but when you were born, he thought you were adorable.'

'He changed his mind?'

'He . . . ' Ruth hesitated again, smiling weakly at Jade, 'he was *overwhelmed* by you.'

'He's got a funny way of showing it,' Jade mumbled.

'He finds it hard to express his emotions, Jade.'

'Tell me something I don't know. He never hugs me.'

Ruth leaned her hand across and rubbed Jade's knee. 'At least he's getting proper treatment now. Dr Michaels seems to think that with the right medication and therapy there's no reason why Dad shouldn't eventually make a full recovery.' She smiled, presuming Jade would be as delighted as she was with such positive news.

But Jade needed more convincing. 'So he'll never trash the shop again or laugh at people dying?'

'Not if he takes the right medicine.'

'And he'll take me to football matches and McDonald's like other dads? And he'll say hello back to people when they say hello to him?'

'Well, yes, hopefully.'

'And he'll stop buying me stupid birthday cards?'

'Oh, not the birthday card thing again!'

'It was stupid!' Jade exclaimed.

Last year, for her eleventh birthday, Goran had sent her a card with a picture of a furry red donkey on it. *Happy Birthday, Dear Nephew*, it had said. She'd made sure it had stayed hidden behind all the others on the mantelpiece.

'He just liked the picture,' Ruth sighed.

But Jade's criteria for judging Goran were different from her mother's. 'Can you promise me he'll buy me a normal card next time? And he'll hug me when I need a hug?' It didn't seem a lot to ask.

'No,' Ruth said, leaning back in her chair, defeated. 'I can't. He'll never be conventional in the way you want, I'm sorry, but he'll . . . he'll give you what he can.'

Give her what he can? What did that mean? Jade struggled to understand what her mother was saying but it didn't make much sense. Why, if the doctor said he'd be better, couldn't he do such small things?

Ruth reached forward for a biscuit and snapped it in half, a light flurry of crumbs raining onto her lap. 'I know you're trying hard, Jade, but I think that there are a lot of things you won't understand until you are even older. Let's just take it a day at a time and see what happens, eh? Jacob's coming over on Thursday. It'll be nice to see him, won't it?' she ended lightly.

'Sure,' Jade said. She went back to reading *The Funday Times* but her eyes were blurred and she felt slightly sick. All the new feelings of sympathy and love she had felt for her father had collapsed, like sandcastles reclaimed by the sea. It all slotted into place now, didn't it? He hadn't even wanted her to be born—Mum had just admitted it. Her father didn't do any of the things other fathers did with their kids, not because of this illness, or because he wasn't 'conventional' but because he didn't love her. Pure and simple. You didn't have to be grown-up to understand *that*.

12

Things were quieter over the next few days, settling into a routine. Jade would sit for long spells at the desk in her bedroom, doodling on pieces of scrap paper or cutting out pictures from magazines. Grandma phoned once, late at night when Jade had been asleep. 'She hasn't found anyone shifty yet, but she's still looking!' Ruth reported.

Sometimes Jade would see the red-haired girl outside the shops. The girl always smiled and Jade smiled back but they hadn't got to the speaking stage yet.

Jade missed Navid and Rosemarie every time she saw the girl. She wondered what they were doing, wondered if they missed her, too. Once, she had started to write to them but she'd screwed the letters up—they wouldn't want to know her now. They wouldn't be interested in someone whose dad was a loony. It didn't matter anyway. She'd make new friends at the High School—maybe meet someone like Molly, who would understand.

Ruth phoned the hospital regularly and updated Jade on Goran's progress. 'He's a lot more lucid now; we talked for a long time,' or 'He's been playing chess with some of the patients; that's a good sign.' Jade would murmur an appropriate response to please her mother. 'Has he mentioned me?' she asked once. 'No, not yet, but he's thinking of you, I'm sure,' Ruth had explained. I'll bet, Jade thought.

After each phone call, Jade could feel her resentment and anger rising and would escape into her room. She would just calm down when Mary Gone-Wrong would arrive in the graveyard, pushing her stupid pram and making things worse. Jade would make a point of scowling down at her, hoping she'd take the hint and get lost but Jade knew she might as well have been invisible. Her stares were no deterrent against nutcases.

She wasn't even looking forward to Jacob's visit; not really. She didn't want Trafalgar Road muddled up with Fleetby-on-the-Hill. Like with home and school, she wanted to keep the two parts separate. But as soon as Jacob arrived, dressed in his synagogue suit despite the summer heat, she changed her mind. No one could resist Jacob. 'Jadey! How you have grown in the countryside air! Like barley! Five inches at least!' he boomed from the doorway, arms outstretched in greeting.

Jade blushed, returning his hug. 'No I haven't!' she protested.

Mr Krazinski glanced excitedly round the cottage. 'Mm, it is like me, small but sweet!'

'You could say that,' Ruth smiled.

'Let me show you my desk,' said Jade enthusiastically, grabbing Jacob's hand.

'Not exactly *your* desk!' Ruth reminded her daughter, but she was already upstairs.

Jacob nodded at the piece of furniture appreciatively. 'Very handsome and very useful, too. Look what I have.' From one of his Krazinski's Continental Bakery carriers he withdrew a large envelope and several letters. 'Postman Pat at your service!'

'Are these all for me?' Jade asked suspiciously, eyeing the unexpected delivery.

'Only if your name is Jade Winter. If it is not, I make big mistake. An old house, this. Very old,' he observed, glancing round.

'Yes.'

'Och! And you have a view over the churchyard. Do the skeletons keep you awake, with all those jangling bones, Jadey? What tune do they play? *"I ain't got no body and no body ain't got me!"* ' he teased.

'No, 'course not!' Jade giggled, glancing at the letters.

'Who is the old lady with the pram?' Jacob asked, bending to peer through the window.

'Oh, just the local nutter,' Jade replied absently.

Jacob stared at the girl in surprise. 'Jade!' he said.

Jade shrugged, pretending she hadn't heard the disapproval in his voice. 'Well, she is, it's obvious.'

Mr Krazinski paused, as if about to say something else, but instead he decided to go downstairs. 'I'll leave you to it, then, and talk with your mother. She says Daddy is making good progress.'

Jade fixed him with her full smile. 'Yes, I know,' she said.

Recognizing instantly the contents of the large brown envelope, she casually dropped it against the side of the desk, determined never to open it. Although it had been less than two weeks since she had left Lorimer Lane, she felt as if she had never been a pupil there. The certificate in the envelope, duplicated and signed in Mrs Gamgee's messy handwriting, meant nothing. The words *Presented to Jade Winter for Outstanding Contribution to the School*, that she guessed were on the certificate, meant even less.

Instead, she concentrated on the remaining letters. The first was from her grandma in Cephalonia.

> *Dear Jade,*
> *Hi there, Trouble! I hope you have settled into Mr Lomas's cottage OK. Have you made new friends there? Remember my advice, won't you?*
> *I wish you could be here with me but on second thoughts, you'd find it too hot—my legs are covered*

in bites—they say midges always go after bad meat!
It is a beautiful island, though, with plenty to see.
Of course I'm eating too much—I hope I don't cause
another earthquake on the island with my weight!
I'll be back next week with lots of prezzies for you
and I hope to find everything a bit more settled?
Lots of love
Grandma
PS Have put this postcard in an envelope so you
should receive it sooner.

Selecting a compartment at the back of the desk, Jade slotted the postcard into it. The desk looked so much better now it had a purpose. She did the same with the remaining, unopened letters, saving them until later. She knew who they were from: Navid, Rosemarie, and Mr Cooper. They confused and pleased her but she didn't feel ready to read them yet. Maybe tonight. Maybe tomorrow. Maybe never.

Stubbornly, she brushed away the tears which had sprung up from nowhere. She didn't want to think about Lorimer Lane. It hurt too much. Carefully, she pulled down the desk lid and ambled downstairs.

In the front room, Jacob insisted on washing up the coffee mugs in the Belfast sink. 'Just like when I was a little boy in Krakow,' he said, delighted by the 'kitchen'.

'Are we ready?' Ruth asked.

'Yep,' Jade replied.

They had not been to visit the hospital for almost a week and Jade could tell from the agitated way Ruth searched for her car keys and had to double-check everything she was nervous and excited. 'It's so nice you're here,' she said to Jacob as they unlocked the car, 'I can stay with him for longer without worrying about Jade.'

'It is my pleasure. I am sorry he is not nearer, so I could come more often,' Jacob said as he levered himself into the passenger seat. 'This Asian flu has been a bad business. Mrs Gamgee had it, you know. It must like teachers and nurses, but luckily not fat shopkeepers,' he informed them merrily, before growing disgruntled at how many times he had to tug the seatbelt over his stomach before it snapped closed. 'Tch! Soon I will have to join the ladies at Weight Watchers, eh?'

'We like you just as you are, Jacob,' Ruth laughed.

At the hospital, Jade searched for Molly but she was not around. 'Maybe her mother has been discharged,' Jacob observed after Jade had explained about her. The possibility hadn't occurred to Jade.

'Can we find out?' she asked, disappointed at the idea of never seeing the older girl again. She had wanted to ask her about things; things she felt only Molly could answer.

Jacob shrugged. 'I don't know. Maybe wait until your mother comes, huh?'

'OK.'

They sat for a while in the reception area, chatting about Church Cottage and the village but as they talked, Jade became aware of a commotion outside. A large blue van had drawn up outside the doors and two guards, like the sort Jade had seen taking money to and from banks, were wrestling with another man. The man was struggling and swearing as the guards tried to drag him inside. By the man's side, a nurse was soothing the distressed patient, trying to calm him with gentle, reassuring words. 'Come, Jadey, let's find that coffee shop I saw a sign for,' Jacob said quietly.

'I don't understand what happens,' Jade said as they settled at a corner table. 'I don't understand why they have to scream and shout so much. It's frightening.'

Jacob stirred his weak coffee with a plastic spoon and sighed. 'Some don't scream and shout, you know? Some go mad quietly, singing softly to themselves. Others just stare at nothing. Staring. Staring. With some people, you can't even tell they are mad. You would think they were perfectly happy until they would do something bizarre.'

'Like running up and down the steps in the middle of the night,' Jade said.

'Or chewing through their own fingers, thinking they were pieces of fruit.'

'Ugh!' Jade said, pushing back the hair she had been about to suck. 'How do you know that, Jacob?'

Jacob took a small sip from the polystyrene cup, furrowing his thick, white eyebrows. 'In the war, I saw many things a boy should never have seen. Bad, obscene things, inhuman things.'

'Done by people like my dad?'

'No! No! Done by soldiers who were sane, who knew what they were doing,' Jacob said sadly. 'And also in the war I saw brave and beautiful things.'

'Who did those?'

'Sometimes other soldiers, sometimes people like your father before he was broken. Does this make sense to you?'

'Not really,' Jade admitted.

'No, nor to me, neither, but that's life. It doesn't always make sense.'

There was a pause. Jacob slurped his coffee noisily, grimacing at the lack of flavour. Jade, remembering Ruth's words from after their long talk last Sunday, looked questioningly into her neighbour's eyes. 'But you saw all these things in the war you were in and you're all right. You're not . . . ' She hesitated, not sure which term to use. Her mother called it 'mental illness'. Grandma had said 'bad with his nerves', Jacob used 'mad', and she had copied Molly's 'nutter'. ' . . . mad or anything,' she concluded.

The baker was about to make a humorous reply but realized the significance of the question. 'No, I'm not mad,' he said.

Her grandma's words, soon after Goran's breakdown, came to her. 'You weren't weak. You kept yourself occupied.'

'It isn't a matter of who is weak or who is strong, princess. That would mean there is a choice. Do you think your daddy chose to be the way he is? Chose to be like Vesuvius? Mmm?'

'No, I guess not.'

'It is not something you can just get rid of with an Anadin tablet.'

'No.'

'Or a cup of Tetley's tea.'

'No.'

'Why do you need to know this? What is bothering you, Jadey?'

'Nothing,' Jade said, lowering her eyes. She focused on the constellation of coffee rings on the table, swallowing hard.

Jacob stretched out his hand, touching Jade's fingertip with his gnarled index finger. 'Your father is a good man, Jade, but he's—'

'Damaged,' Jade interrupted. 'I understand that. I know it's because of what happened to him when he was small and everything. I just don't know why he's damaged with me. I've always tried to be a good girl.'

'You are a good girl! A very good girl,' Jacob agreed.

'I'm not rude to him or naughty or anything. And I've never been grounded. Navid's always being grounded,' Jade continued, in full flow now, despite knowing Jacob didn't really understand what she was saying.

'Ah, that Navid! Always asking me for free samples! Cheeky boy!' Jacob nodded.

'So why doesn't my dad love me?' Jade asked suddenly.

The question disarmed her listener totally. 'Sure he loves you!' her mentor protested. 'All fathers love their little girls!'

'No they don't!' Jade replied heatedly, frustrated that he was trying to fob her off with such pat phrases that were patently untrue.

'Has he once hit you or hurt you in any way?' Jacob persisted.

'No. So?'

'No, he is a gentle man.'

Jade sighed heavily, regretting her outburst. Better to say nothing, like she had at school. Better to keep things to yourself so you don't end up feeling and looking stupid, like she did now. Jacob scratched his head, saddened by the weary expression on the face opposite him. A weariness that he felt had no right to be part of an eleven-year-old's countenance at all. 'My father never told me he loved me. Not once,' he revealed.

'Didn't he?' Jade asked, interested. Maybe, like Molly, they shared common ground.

'But he showed me, in lots of ways,' the baker continued.

'Well then, that's where we're different,' Jade mumbled.

Defeated, Jacob braved another sip of his coffee. 'Maybe when you are older,' he began.

'Yeah. Yeah, when I'm older.' Jade shrugged indifferently.

'Who is this girl in front of me?' Jacob suddenly announced, banging his hand down onto the table with a 'thwack!' and looking round for an answer to his question.

'Jacob!' Jade said, unsure whether to laugh or be embarrassed.

'Has anyone seen Jade Winter?' he demanded sourly. A young man on the next table, munching through a cherry muffin, shook his head.

'Excuse me, young girl,' Jacob said directly to Jade, pretending to rise, 'I am going to have to ask you to leave. You are imposter!'

'Give up, Jacob, you know I'm not!'

'I think so! My Jade does not feel so sorry for herself. My Jade counts her blessings. She knows she has a nice home. She knows she has many, many people who love and cherish her. She knows she has so much talent, people come calling to her, begging her sell it to them!'

'Jacob, stop it, please,' Jade protested, her face burning.

'Who are you?' he demanded, eyes flashing.

'I am Jade.'

'My Jade?'

'Your Jade.'

Slowly, Jacob lowered himself into his seat, his voice returning to its normal, comforting pitch. He patted her hand again. 'Good girl. You are lucky, eh? You have so many good things in your life—letters from friends, prizes at school, good-looking neighbours who bake the best cinnamon buns in Europe.' Here, Jacob stroked his wiry hair like a vain film star, waiting for her to return the compliment but Jade only managed the slightest of smiles. A note of seriousness returned to his voice. 'It is bad, what happened. I did not like you saw your daddy in the street but there are worse things than that. He did not do it on purpose. He needed help.'

For a while, Jade did not respond. Instead, she stared thoughtfully at the cuffs of Jacob's shirt. They were starched and clean but very frayed. His suit, too, on close inspection, had a worn sheen to it she would not normally have noticed. They were not the clothes of a rich man, despite Jacob Krazinski's years of hard work in the bakery, but they were the clothes of an old-fashioned, respectful man, who wore a suit to a hospital visit because, in his eyes, that was the right thing to do. They were the clothes of a good man.

'I wish you had been my dad's dad. He'd have been all right then,' Jade finally stated.

'He'd have been fatter, I can tell you that!' Jacob laughed.

'And you would have been my grandad,' she added shyly.

'Oh! I am that anyway, in everything but name, aren't I?'

'I guess,' Jade agreed, grinning.

'You are OK now?'

'Yes, you've helped a lot,' Jade replied softly. He had helped her to see that even if her father didn't—or couldn't—show his love for her, others did. And that made her feel special. She was lucky. But she still didn't feel whole.

'No more calling little old ladies names, eh?' Jacob continued. 'You know better. That was not you. Who was that girl?'

Ashamed, Jade whispered, 'I don't know.'

'Remember—you are a bright, beautiful girl and you have a choice.'

Jade nodded as Jacob pushed his cup to one side.

'Just as I am choosing not to drink this muck.'

Ruth arrived then, a tight smile on her face. 'You can go up to see Goran, if you like, Jacob, but maybe for only a few minutes? He finds it hard to talk for long—the medicine, you know?'

'I know,' Jacob replied, rising to allow Ruth to take his seat.

Jade fetched her mother a hot chocolate from the counter, careful to avoid eye contact with the other customers, especially the muffin-eater, on her return. 'How's Dad?' she asked.

Ruth shrugged. She looked pale and drawn. 'Oh, better, I guess, but tired still. It's going to take a long time.'

'What was he doing?' Jade asked.

'Just lying in bed.'

'Well, that's got to be better than throwing things about and talking to invisible people,' Jade pointed out.

'I guess so.'

Jade could sense her mother's disappointment and realized too, how little she received in the way of affection from Goran. Molly's insensitive but accurate words echoed in her head. 'Mental people are the worst to live with— that's cos they're mental!' Goran was difficult to live with, would always be difficult to live with, but he was a husband and father, nevertheless. And Jacob was right— he had never hit them or even shouted at them in his life. He was a gentle person, struggling to make sense of the world, like everybody else. He just wasn't very good at it sometimes. Like her mother said, he gave what he could. 'Do you think he'll be ready to come down soon so I can see him?' Jade asked.

Ruth glanced at her. 'Are you ready?' she asked searchingly.

Jade shrugged. 'As ready as I'll ever be, I suppose.'

That night, when the old woman wheeled her pram into the graveyard, Jade sat well back from the window, listening intently, trying to make sense of the ranting and spitting. Trying to understand.

13

'Y ou, young lady, need some new clothes and a haircut,' Ruth said as she watched Jade brushing her hair the next morning.

'I'm growing it for secondary,' Jade protested, frowning at her mother through the reflection in the mirror.

'And that's another thing,' her mother said, clearing the cereal bowls away. 'Do you realize you'll be at the High School in five weeks?'

'Yes,' Jade replied, wondering where this sudden interest in her school life had come from.

'I couldn't believe it when I was checking through my diary this morning. Your dad's due out on the twenty-first, all being well, and you start two weeks later. We'll need to get your uniform sorted—and new shoes and a bag and games kit. God! I don't suppose we brought that list with us the school sent, did we?'

'It's on the pin board at home. I've already got the tie and sweatshirt, though, remember? You bought it on that Open Evening so there's no rush.'

Ruth sighed. 'I can't believe you're starting secondary school. My little baby!'

Jade strode up to her mother, standing directly in front of her. The top of her head reached her mother's chin. 'Not that little!' she declared.

'You'll be borrowing my clothes next.'

'I'm not that sad either!' Jade announced. 'These are what I like.' She flicked open her copy of *Sugar* magazine and pointed to an array of summery outfits being modelled by skinny teenagers.

Ruth screwed up her nose. 'What are those designers thinking? Still, I wore some pretty foul outfits when I was that age. Your grandad used to have a dicky fit!'

'What about Grandma?'

'Oh, Grandma was worse than me! Always a bit of a fashion victim, our Sheila. Between you and me, I think she's a frustrated supermodel. Ah well. Come on, scruffy lass, let's get you kitted out. North Bellwood looks big enough to have a few decent shops at least.'

North Bellwood was very busy with Saturday shoppers but that just added to Jade's excitement. It had been months and months since she'd been shopping for clothes with her mother.

Today, nothing seemed too expensive or too gaudy for Ruth. She allowed Jade to select her own clothes and shoes, not once mentioning the outrageous price or the height of the heels or the lousy workmanship. 'Can we afford all this, Mum?' Jade asked during a break for coffee.

''Course we can. This is our holiday, remember? I don't want your only memory of it being spent in a hospital reception area. Relax and enjoy!'

'What about you? Are you going to buy anything?'

'No. I'm going to wait and see how your dad is. I thought if you were OK I'd take him off somewhere at half-term while you stayed with Grandma.'

'Fine by me.'

Ruth drained the remains of her coffee and donned her sunglasses. 'Right then, madam. Where next?'

'School bag?'

'School bag. That shouldn't be a problem.'

But it was. On this instance, Ruth was adamant that

Jade should have something well crafted and made of leather, not the canvas sports type Jade wanted. 'We'll try one more shop, then we'll leave it until another time,' Ruth stated testily.

'Let's go in here, then,' Jade said, attracted by the loud, thudding music coming from within a shop called Big Fat Zero. Ruth sighed. 'I'm over-aged to go in here,' she complained, following her daughter through the door.

Big Fat Zero was crowded, full of teenagers huddled in chatty groups or individuals like Jade, accompanied by reluctant parents complaining of the ridiculousness of the prices. Suddenly, Jade heard a shriek and saw the unmistakable bleached head of Molly Hepworth by the shoe and bag section. 'There's Molly, Mum!' Jade cried. 'Come on.'

Jade fought her way through to Molly, too overjoyed at seeing her to feel shy in front of her companions. 'Molly, it's me, Jade,' she said, tugging the girl's arm.

Molly's eyebrows shot to the top of her forehead. 'Hiya, kid. What you doing here?' she grinned.

'I'm with my mum. We're trying to find a bag for high school.'

'*Trying* being the appropriate word,' Ruth said, smiling grimly.

'Oh, we'll get you sorted, won't we?' Molly said. She pointed to a youth with dark, greased-back hair and a dagger tattooed on his neck. 'Darren'll serve you. He works here.' Darren nodded coolly. 'He's Kell's bloke,' Molly explained, throwing her arm around 'Kell', a slight, rabbity-faced girl with identically tattooed neck.

'What sort of bag do you want?' Darren asked.

Kelly nudged Molly in the ribs. 'In't he professional?' she noted proudly.

'Something sturdy,' Ruth intervened. 'Made of leather, preferably.'

'Leather! What you trying to do? Cripple her? She wants something light—those text books weigh a ton, you know!' Molly said. 'Show her those over there, young man.'

Darren obediently headed for a display of large canvas bags, exactly the sort Jade had wanted. Ruth rolled her eyes. 'Here,' she said, handing Jade some money. 'I'm going to buy your dad a pair of pyjamas from Bhs across the road then I'll be on that bench outside when you've finished.' She smiled at Molly. 'Nice meeting you, Molly.'

'Ditto.'

Ruth turned and fought her way through the shop.

'She seems all right,' Molly said as they waited for Darren to unhook the bags from the display.

'She is.'

'It helps when one of 'em's normal.'

'That's true,' Jade acknowledged. 'How's yours?' she asked, keeping her voice low in case Molly had anything bad to report.

'Oh, she's discharged herself early, silly cow,' Molly replied.

'She's great, your mum,' Kelly admonished, 'don't call her a cow.'

Molly shrugged. 'She's my mum, I'll call her what I want—the silly cow!'

'Take no notice,' Kelly said, speaking directly to Jade, 'Mo loves her to bits—go on, admit it.'

''Course I do—never said otherwise, did I? She can still be a silly cow though, can't she? Now, are we going to choose this girl the best bag, or what? She wants one that says, "don't mess with me, guys, for I am Top Banana!"'

For ten minutes, Kelly, Darren, and Molly discussed the merits of one bag over another until finally they narrowed it down to two styles. 'You get final choice, kid,' Molly said.

'That's big of you!' Kelly laughed.

Jade smiled, thinking how easy-going she was. 'I'll have that one,' she decided, indicating the largest of the two, 'it's got more pouches for stuff.'

'That's the one I would have picked,' Molly agreed. They came across to the counter to help Jade pay. There was a long queue, so Kelly said she would wait by the window.

'She's nice,' Jade said.

'All my friends are nice. They wouldn't be friends otherwise, would they?' Molly said simply.

Jade hesitated. 'Does she know about your mum being—you know . . . '

'A suicide freak? 'Course she does—she's my best mate. I tell her everything.'

They moved closer to the till. 'Don't you mind her knowing?'

'Mind? 'Course not. That's what friends are for, isn't it? God! I couldn't keep all that mess to myself, I'd end up as mental as me mam!'

'What about other people—you know—the ones you said stared at you from behind their net curtains.'

Molly snorted. 'Who cares?' She sniffed, reaching into her pocket for a piece of chewing gum which she offered to Jade first, before cramming the rest into her mouth. 'I suppose if I'm honest it did use to bother me, when I was a sprog like you—no offence—but I've learned that everyone's got someone bent in their family, so no one's got room to talk. Miss Spivey told me one person in seven has mental problems. That's about,' she paused, scrutinizing the customers, 'about six people in here, right now. Like I always say, no one's perfect.'

'That explains Mary Poppins,' Jade said.

'Come again?'

Briefly, Jade explained about the old woman in St Cecilia's. 'Oh, you mean Miss Hesketh!' Molly said, shuffling forward in the queue.

'You know her?' Jade asked in amazement.

'Everyone knows her, she's legendary.'

There was no time to ask more questions as they had reached the front of the queue. Jade handed over the cash and watched as the cashier dropped her new bag into an opaque carrier. There was hardly any change. 'Oh, well, I guess it's wet hanky time,' Molly said.

'Pardon?' Jade asked.

'Goodbye, kid.'

'Oh, yes, I guess,' Jade replied, crestfallen. It surprised her how sad she felt at the thought of not seeing Molly again, someone she had only met twice, after all.

Presumably, Molly felt the same because she pushed her way back to the paying desk and whistled shrilly for attention. 'Hey, pass me one of those,' Molly demanded, pointing to a flyer for an open air concert behind the cashier's head.

'You could say please,' the girl sniffed.

'Yeah, I could,' Molly retorted before instructing Jade to turn round.

'What are you doing?' Jade asked, as something tickled her back.

'Hold still, will you,' Molly replied. 'There!'

She flashed the sheet under Jade's nose. 'My address. You can drop me a line and we can compare nut stories. I'll win, obviously.'

Jade squinted. 'My dad would die if he saw your writing,' she announced, secretly delighted by the gift. 'What's that underneath?'

'June fifteenth. My birthday, of course. Anything alcoholic will do.'

Jade laughed, then caught a brief glimpse of her mother sitting on the bench outside. 'Wait here,' she said.

'Where else is there?' the bemused girl retorted.

'You could try the Oxfam shop,' the cashier sneered beneath her breath. As Molly turned to give the girl a mouthful, Jade dashed out of the shop.

'Mum, I need money!' Jade announced.

'How much?' Ruth asked, opening her purse.

Jade snatched a five pound note from the back. 'That'll do! Wait here.'

'Yes, miss.'

There was a newsagent's next to Bhs with exactly what Jade was looking for.

'Wait here,' she repeated as she darted breathlessly past Ruth, who was staring bewilderedly into Big Fat Zero's window.

'Here you go,' Jade said, thrusting a box of chocolates into Molly's hand.

'You're mad, you are!' Molly protested, blushing.

Jade grinned broadly. 'Do you remember in the waiting room at Bellwood, you said nobody ever buys us chocolates, the Jade Winters and the Molly Hepworths of this world?'

The Molly Hepworth of the world shrugged. 'Did I?'

'Yeah, you did. Well, now someone has!' Jade laughed.

Molly flipped the box over, to read the contents. 'Just looking to see how many nut ones there are!'

'One in seven, isn't it?' Jade quipped.

'Yeah, one in seven,' Molly smiled, her eyes glinting.

'Jade,' Ruth called, 'we need to be going.'

'See you then, kid,' Molly said, wiping her eyes with the back of her hand.

'Yeah, see you, Molly. Thanks,' Jade replied, heading for the door.

'Tell Miss Spivey I'll give her that fifty p. back next time!' Molly yelled as an afterthought.

Outside, Ruth divided the packages between the two of them and they headed for the car park. 'So that was the famous Molly,' Ruth said.

'Yeah.'

'She seemed very . . . bubbly.'

'She is.'

'Don't go getting any ideas about nose studs, will you?'

'As if. I like her for the things she says, not for what she looks like.'

'Oh,' Ruth said, glancing sideways at her daughter. 'And what does she have to say that's so intriguing?'

'Well, she just knows about stuff,' Jade replied.

'Like what?'

'Like nobody's perfect.'

'I could have told you that.'

Jade thought about it for a moment. 'It's not the same coming from you,' she said, trying to be honest.

Ruth laughed. 'No, I don't suppose it is, High School Girl!'

'Old woman.'

'Teeny-bopper.'

'Geriatric.'

'Geriatric? Watch it, buster!' Ruth aimed her armful of carriers at Jade who dodged smartly out of her way.

'See, you can't even aim straight,' she mocked, galloping ahead to the car before her mother could take revenge.

On the journey home, Ruth ticked off all the things they'd bought out loud. 'All you really need now is your writing equipment and we can just pop into our shop for that.'

'Yes, I know. Navid and Rosemarie are always going on about how jammy I am, living above a shop,' Jade revealed.

'Invite them round when we get back. They can choose too from what's left of the stock.'

'Maybe,' Jade said vaguely.

'Maybe,' Ruth repeated, imitating Jade's evasive response. 'Do you realize that every time I mention them you try to change the subject, Jade. Have you had an argument with them?'

'No.'

'Is that why you missed the last few days of school?'

'No!' Jade mumbled.

'What then?'

'Nothing.' Why did Ruth have to bring all this up now? They'd had a great day—the best in years—and now she was spoiling it all.

Sensing her daughter's withdrawal, Ruth tactfully changed the subject. 'Hey! Why don't we go to the pub tonight? Have a slap up meal à la Black Bull?'

'OK,' Jade agreed, grateful her mother hadn't tried to lead the conversation further. She knew she had come a long way, but memories of the end of term were still difficult to talk about. Like her father, she was a little bit damaged.

Upstairs, Jade dropped her new purchases on her bed, leaving all but her bag in the carriers. This, her one reminder of Molly, she reverently placed in the top drawer beneath the desk, planning to get it out again first thing in the morning and examine every tiny detail. As she closed the drawer, she caught sight of the unopened letters

Jacob had brought on Thursday. Tentatively, she reached out for Rosemarie's, but as she began to open it, Ruth shouted upstairs to tell her The Bull had only got early bookings left and they had to leave immediately if they wanted to eat. Sighing heavily, Jade replaced the letter in the back of the desk and went downstairs.

14

The Black Bull was already full of diners, mainly outsiders from town, attracted to its village setting and 'fine country ales'. The harassed landlord apologized, saying the only table he could offer would have to be shared, unless they minded waiting until much later. Ruth declined to wait, saying they were starving, and they were escorted to a table by a wide inglenook fireplace. Mrs Lunn from the village shop, mid-way through her prawn cocktail, looked up at them in surprise. 'Sorry, Lottie,' the landlord said, 'we're bursting at the seams tonight.'

Jade groaned inwardly. She already felt uncomfortable in the alien surroundings of the restaurant without having to sit opposite that miserable old bat. However, as they took their seats, Mrs Lunn smiled broadly, much to Jade's astonishment. 'I recommend the lemon sole,' she said to Ruth, who was scouring the menu.

'Mm, I think I need something more challenging than that,' Ruth replied. 'A good piece of lamb or pork fillet, perhaps.'

Within seconds they were yammering on in the annoying way adults had of being able to talk about the most boring stuff ever. 'So how are you getting on with Miss Hesketh?' Mrs Lunn eventually asked.

'Miss Hesketh?'

'Annie, next door but one, bless her. You must have seen her, pushing her pram around.'

'Oh, yes, of course. We haven't had much to do with her, actually,' Ruth replied.

'She's in the graveyard a lot. I've seen her from my bedroom window,' Jade added.

Mrs Lunn nodded, pushing her glass dish to the edge of the table, ready for collection. 'You mustn't take any notice of her in the graveyard. She's harmless.'

'I feel I'm missing something here. What does she do?' Ruth asked.

'Spits on the graves,' Jade said.

'Only on the one grave, I think you'll find,' Mrs Lunn corrected her.

'What for?' Ruth wanted to know.

Lottie Lunn paused, waiting for the waitress to first jot down Ruth and Jade's order, then take away her dish. 'It's a long story. Are you sure you want to hear it?'

Ruth smiled politely, sending Jade a signal of apology by kicking her lightly on the shins as if to say 'Sorry, pet, we'll have to humour her,' but Jade was genuinely curious. 'My friend says she's legendary,' Jade announced.

Mrs Lunn wiped her chin daintily. 'Well, I don't know about that but she does have a long history. Annie Hesketh was an assistant teacher here during the war. I didn't know her, but my mother did. A real beauty she was, by all accounts—Annie, that is, not my mother—plain as a water biscuit, my mother.'

She paused to smile at her own joke before continuing. 'Anyway, Annie fell for Wilfred Whitehead, the heir to Fleetby Hall—that was demolished in the sixties to make way for the Hemplands housing estate—terrible waste but that was the sixties for you. Soon enough, Annie "found herself with child".' Mrs Lunn paused to clear her throat and glance at Jade, as if checking it was all right to discuss such things, before continuing. 'At first, Wilfred was going to marry her, against his father George's wishes, but George made him promise to wait until after the baby was born.'

'Why?' Jade asked.

'I don't know, duck. They were peculiar about such stuff in those days. Anyway, Annie was sent off to a nursing home and Wilfred was sent off to fight at Dunkirk—not that *he* saw much action over there by all accounts. The action started when he came home on leave and he started courting somebody else—Elizabeth Claremont her name was. Now she did get his father's approval; from the same drawer, you see—'

'Same drawer?' Jade asked.

'Same class. Same amount of money.'

'Oh.'

'Then, of course, Annie turned up with the baby and it caused a bit of a problem, especially with the complications.'

'Complications?'

'The baby was a mongol,' Mrs Lunn whispered.

'Down's Syndrome,' Ruth corrected her.

'So?' Jade said. There were two Down's Syndrome pupils at Lorimer Lane. They needed extra attention in class but otherwise played, worked, argued, and swore like everyone else.

'Wilfred denied all knowledge of it; said the baby couldn't possibly belong to him, with his pedigree. Didn't want a handicapped baby inheriting Fleetby Hall.'

'That's horrible!' Jade said hotly.

'I agree with you,' Mrs Lunn said, leaning back to allow her main course to be placed in front of her. 'But you haven't heard the worst of it.'

'Why? What happened?'

'According to my mother, who ran the post office before me and so knew everything, George had Annie and the baby taken away to a mental asylum; they could do that in those days—incarcerate people on no grounds at all.'

109

'It doesn't bear thinking about,' Ruth said softly.

'Then what happened?' Jade asked.

'Wilfred married Elizabeth but they never had any children,' Mrs Lunn replied.

Jade leaned across, captivated. 'Not to them. To Annie, to the baby?'

'He died when he was a toddler. Heart trouble, I think.'

'Oh, poor thing!' Jade cried.

'I know, it's a shame. Annie never recovered. She was locked up for years in Bellwood—it's a general hospital now but the old part of it used to be the asylum. People still call it the loony bin, you know. Some of the older locals won't even go to have their bunions lanced in case they're chucked in a padded cell.'

Jade and Ruth exchanged brief glances but didn't interrupt. 'Anyway, years and years later they let Miss Hesketh out into the community. I think that did her more harm than good. She made her way straight back to Fleetby and rented the house nearest to Wilfred she could get—right opposite his grave!'

'Doesn't she have any help from social services?' Ruth asked. 'Her house seems very run-down.'

'She gets taken to Day Care at Bellwood on Mondays and she has meals on wheels. Her house is as clean as a pin inside—I put it down to all those years of regimentation in the hospital—it's them kids from the Hemplands who keep breaking her windows. They want birching, the lot of them,' Mrs Lunn stated, looking straight at Jade.

Jade blushed and lowered her eyes, remembering all the times she had stared belligerently at the old lady from her bedroom window.

The waitress arrived, bringing Ruth and Jade their orders. Mrs Lunn, having finished her own meal, wished them a good evening and left. 'Well,' Ruth said, tucking straight in to her dish, 'and I told Jacob this was a nice quiet village where nothing much happened!'

Jade toyed with the chicken curry she had ordered, her appetite deserting her. 'I don't get it, Mum. So they locked her up when there was nothing wrong with her and they let her out when she was . . . damaged?'

Her mother nodded, concentrating on her lamb cutlet. 'Don't worry; you can't just slam people in an institution now because they inconvenience you. We've come a long way since those days, Jade.'

'But shouldn't she still be in there if she's mad?'

'Who's to say she is mad? If that had happened to me I'd be doing more than spitting on graves, I can tell you.'

'Me too!' Jade stared thoughtfully at her rapidly cooling meal. 'It's like you said about Dad—there's always a reason.'

Ruth pointed a fork at Jade's plate. 'Come on, girlie— dig in.'

Jade tried a few mouthfuls of the curry but her mind was whirring. 'Why are people so cruel?' she asked.

'Which people?'

'Like Dad's stepfather and Wilfred Whitehead and people Jacob knew in the war and . . .'

Ruth laid her hand gently on her daughter's. 'Jade, please. I know what you're saying is important but let's lighten up a bit, eh? We've got Dad to visit together tomorrow, so that's going to be stressful enough.'

Jade stared in surprise at her mother. Usually, she was the one who wanted to avoid the issue or change the subject, not Ruth. 'Is everything all right, Mum?' she asked.

Unable to look directly at Jade, Ruth concentrated on cutting the bone from the middle of her cutlet. 'I just want to enjoy this meal, my big girl—seeing you bound into that trendy shop today, full of confidence, brought home how little time I've got left with you.'

'I'm not going to snuff it, Mum!'

'I meant before you start ignoring me. Gadding off every Saturday with your friends, eyeing up the lads, giving me grief over the telephone bill. Growing up, in other words,' Ruth explained, trying to keep her voice light but failing.

'If it's about the bag,' Jade began.

Ruth shook her head, smiling fondly now at her daughter. 'No, no, you were right about the bag—it just showed how out of touch I was. It's a bit of a shock when you find out your opinion comes second to spotty kids' with frizzy bleached hair!'

'I hope I get spots soon,' Jade said. 'I'll know I'm growing up then!'

'That's the sign, is it?' Ruth grinned.

'That and periods.'

'Oh, don't,' Ruth teased, reaching for her glass. 'I've only just recovered from changing your nappies.'

'Get real, Mum!' Jade protested. She paused for a moment, absent-mindedly snapping pieces from the edge of her discarded poppadom. 'But I guess I'm not that grown-up yet or I'd be calling you a silly cow.'

Ruth spluttered with laughter, spraying wine all over the tablecloth.

'Everything all right, madam?' the landlord asked in a concerned voice.

'We're fine,' Ruth managed to reply, frantically mopping the damp linen. 'We'll have the bill please.'

Later, Jade lay restlessly on top of her sleeping bag, listening to the crickets in the graveyard. It was a comforting sound, one she would always associate with her short time in Church Cottage. She would miss living here, in this quiet world, but the discussion with her mother had made her realize just how much she missed home, despite the episode with her father. Missed waving to Jacob as she passed Krazinski's window on the way to school. Missed the bustle of Trafalgar Road, despite the traffic and litter and noise. Most of all, how much she missed her friends. Finally, this evening, she had opened the letters.

Mr Cooper had scribbled a short note, saying he was sorry she'd been unable to attend the Leavers' Service and hoped everything was OK. He was sad not to have said goodbye to her and invited her to drop him a note at home, if she felt like it. He had put a question mark and left a gap, as if to say: 'I'm not being pushy—you don't have to if you don't want to.' She sighed regretfully, wondering how much *Harry Potter* would cost to post.

Navid's letter had been even shorter than Mr Cooper's—but then he was allergic to writing. 'Typical Leeds United fan,' it read in block capitals, 'never there for the final. Give me a ring when you get back. Nav.'

Her letter from Rosemarie had been the opposite—covering pages and pages of notepaper. The first page mentioned Goran straightaway. She'd heard about what happened from her mum who had heard about it from Jacob. 'Hope your dad gets better soon—can I send him a card?' she had wanted to know. The rest of the letter was full of questions: When are you coming back? You will sit with me on the bus to the High School, won't you? Have you got your bus pass yet? Guess what my dad's done to his car? Ordinary, regular questions from one friend to another.

The letters made her feel brilliant. Rosemarie and Navid still liked her, still wanted to be her friends, despite the fact Goran was weird with them when they visited and was now on a psychiatric ward.

Molly's strident voice echoed in her ear. ''Course they do, dumbo—they're your mates! Get a life!'

Jade smiled and turned over to go to sleep.

15

Jade was so engrossed in replying to her letters the next morning, she didn't hear Ruth enter her bedroom. 'You look busy,' her mother said cheerfully.

'I am,' Jade replied, putting on a newsreader's voice. 'I'm catching up with my correspondence and do not wish to be disturbed.'

Ruth stared in amusement at the array of sheets strewn across the desk. 'What was in the big envelope? I've been dying to know,' she asked casually.

Jade glanced sideways at the package still propped against the desk. 'Oh, I haven't opened that yet.'

'Why?'

'It's only that merit award—you've seen loads of them at home when Dad fills them in. They're no big deal.'

'They are when my daughter receives one,' Ruth murmured. She knelt down beside Jade's chair so that she could look directly into her eyes. 'I was so proud when you told us you'd been awarded the prize for Outstanding Contribution. "That's the one", your dad always says, "that's the most special. That's the one that shows character *and* intelligence."'

'Does he?'

'Aha.'

'I'm not sure about it, now,' Jade said, frowning at the envelope.

'What do you mean?' Ruth asked.

Jade nibbled the inside of her lip thoughtfully. 'It doesn't . . . it doesn't mean as much.'

'Because you didn't go to the service?'

'I suppose so. It's sort of spoilt it.'

'Don't let it. You worked hard for that award. And how do you think it will make Dad feel if he knew he'd ruined it for you? It would break his heart.'

'Would it?'

'Yes. And mine.'

Ruth reached for Jade, holding her tight for a long time before being distracted by how untidy her daughter's bed was. 'Not to mention Grandma's,' she added, striding across and shaking the sleeping bag into submission.

Jade laughed. 'And everyone at Weight Watchers.'

Ruth snorted 'And the whole population of Cephalonia and all Greek islands in a hundred mile radius! She's bound to have told everyone she meets.'

Jade glanced thoughtfully at her mother. 'Gran doesn't really understand about Dad's illness, does she? She says nobody in Yorkshire had nervous breakdowns but Molly told me one in seven people has some sort of mental illness so even Yorkshire people must.'

'Of course they do.'

'Maybe she'll understand when she's older,' Jade joked. She stared at her name written in Mrs Gamgee's spidery scrawl across the large envelope her mother had propped against the desk. 'I could take it in to show to Dad this afternoon,' she suggested.

Ruth followed her gaze. 'That would be lovely—it's something special to share with him,' Ruth agreed.

'You don't think he'll get upset again, do you? You know, cry about the printing?'

Ruth glanced at Mrs Gamgee's handwriting. 'He might, but for the right reasons this time!' she said.

* * *

116

Jade clamped the large envelope to her side as she walked through the doors of the reception area. It was busier today, crowded out with buggies and toddlers running round while irate parents snapped at them to behave.

Janet Spivey was on desk duty, trying not to appear harassed by the mayhem, as Ruth enquired about Goran. 'He thought he might be up to meeting us in the Day Room this time,' she explained.

Janet nodded in agreement. 'I think you'll find he's already there waiting for you,' she said. 'Through the doors on the left and along the corridor.'

'Thank you,' Ruth said, gathering her carriers full of clean underwear and new pyjamas for her husband.

'Molly says she'll pay you that fifty p. she owes you next time she sees you,' Jade yelled over her shoulder.

'That'll be the day!' Janet called after her.

Jade dashed after Ruth, struggling to keep up with her brisk pace. Her stomach churned as reality sank in. This was it, then? No more hanging around near the drink machine. No more sitting with Jacob in the coffee bar. No Molly bounding in to save the day. No more postponements. She was going to come face to face with her father and she had no idea what to expect.

She knew Goran wouldn't be crazy; shouting or screaming or talking to himself. In fact, Ruth had warned her, he might be the opposite, quiet and remote. But what would she say to him? What would he say to her?

The churning threatened to develop into something worse. A strong, acidic taste filled her mouth but she forced herself to swallow. What was wrong? She had been fine up to now. Laughing and joking in the car. Planning how she would present the envelope. Prepared. But now . . .

She had to go through with this. She had to. What would Molly do? Just go in and say, *'Hey up, Dad, you look foul!'* or something. But she wasn't Molly.

A nurse brushed past her, knocking her elbow accidentally. 'Mum, hang on,' Jade said as they neared the end of the corridor.

Ruth turned, glancing questioningly, waiting for an explanation.

'Can we just sit here for a minute?' she asked, indicating an empty row of plastic orange chairs a few yards from the entrance to the Day Room.

'What's wrong?'

'I feel sick and . . . and I've got something in my trainer.' Promptly, she sat down on the nearest seat and slowly undid her laces, aware that, yet again, she was delaying the moment when she had to see him.

'He's expecting us,' Ruth reminded her gently.

'I know,' Jade replied, concentrating hard on her laces. The truth was, despite everything she had learned from Ruth and Jacob and Molly, when it came to the crunch, she was still uncertain about her feelings towards her father.

And she knew exactly why she was uncertain. Because she still felt he didn't love her, and because of that, she didn't think she loved him. And if she didn't love her father, what sort of a person did that make her? Was she wicked? Always running errands for everybody else but not even wanting to see her own flesh and blood. Was she that nasty Jade Winter Jacob warned her about?

Clumsily, she tipped out an imaginary stone from her shoe, retying her lace with an ever-decreasing speed. Maybe, like her mother had said, there were some things that she just wouldn't understand until she was older.

'All set?' Ruth asked.

'Tell me again why he didn't want children,' Jade suddenly asked.

Ruth collapsed heavily onto the chair next to Jade. 'I never said he didn't want *you*,' she began tiredly.

'I know that. I said *why* didn't he want children.'

'Because he thought it was wrong to bring children in to the world when it was such a lousy place.'

'And is it wrong?'

Ruth was finding it difficult to keep patient. 'God, Jade, you do choose your moments for philosophical debates!' she said exasperatedly, unable to understand Jade's sudden change in attitude. 'No, of course it's not wrong,' she said firmly.

'Why isn't it wrong?'

'Because if it were wrong, you wouldn't be here and the world would be without the most precious thing in it,' Ruth said earnestly.

'I'm not the—' Jade began.

'You are to me, and your dad, and your grandma,' Ruth interrupted, anticipating her response. She sighed heavily, glancing from Jade's troubled eyes towards the swing doors of the Day Room. 'You wait here. I'll take Dad his pyjamas and then we'll go home. You're obviously not ready yet, and it won't do anybody any good if you go in like this. Don't move, OK?'

Jade stared at the ground miserably and waited, immune to the murmur of voices which rose and fell, a snapshot of sound, as the Day Room door opened and closed.

'Jade,' a voice said.

She didn't reply.

'Jade,' the voice repeated.

Slowly, Jade looked up. Her father towered above her, looking down on her with puzzled, watery eyes. 'Hello, Dad,' she said hesitantly, then after a long pause, 'Why don't you sit with me?'

Cautiously, he did so, lowering himself gradually with the unsure, fragile movements of a much older man. 'I'm still a bit shaky,' he explained.

'You will be,' Jade replied, disconcerted by how simple the meeting was, in the end. She cleared her throat, taking time to adjust to his presence. Now and again, she would dart glances at him shyly, uncomfortably, noting his gaunt face was cleanly-shaven and tender. He smelt, unusually, of tobacco and almonds.

'This isn't a good place to be,' he said.

'You'll be home soon,' Jade reassured him.

'I meant for you. It's not a place for children.'

'I'm fine, Dad, honest.'

He sighed heavily. 'You have something to show me?' he asked presently.

Nodding, Jade held out the unopened envelope for him to take. His hand was shaking slightly. 'I'll open it, shall I?' she asked.

'Please.'

Unsteadily, she withdrew the certificate from its stiff envelope. The design was familiar to both of them, although she was surprised by how pleased she felt when she saw her name, in large, carefully rounded letters along the dotted line. Mrs Gamgee had obviously spent a long time on it. She cared, too.

'Not bad,' the calligrapher pronounced.

Did he mean the handwriting or the award itself? Jade wondered. 'Thanks,' she replied.

'It's better through here—they have drinks, softer chairs,' Goran said, indicating the Day Room behind him.

'OK,' Jade agreed.

Without another word, he stood up and pushed open the door, holding it for her to pass through. It was only a small gesture; something most adults would have done automatically, but for Goran, it was a big step. 'Thanks, Dad,' she beamed.

He shrugged. He was giving her what he could.

'You did great,' Ruth said on the way home.

'I just sat there mainly,' Jade said modestly.

'He listened to you though. He was interested when you told him about the desk.'

'Yes, he was, wasn't he? I'll draw it for him when we get back, so I can take it to him tomorrow.'

'Tomorrow will be easier,' Ruth assured her.

16

Jade was restless when they got back to the cottage. It was early evening and still warm. 'Do you fancy a walk?' she asked Ruth.

Ruth screwed her nose up. 'Not really. I just want to veg out and drink tea and eat biscuits.'

'Don't work too hard, will you?' Jade sniffed.

'Do you know what you've stopped doing?' Ruth observed.

'What?'

'Chewing your hair.'

Immediately, Jade fed a thick clump of it into her mouth and started sucking.

'Oh, ha, ha!'

Jade spat the strand out, then grinned. 'I'm going to post my letters, I may be some time,' she declared mysteriously.

'As you wish, ma'am,' Ruth replied, snuggling down into her armchair and reaching for her magazine.

Jade sauntered along the main street, past the deserted churchyard and rows of quiet, mellowed houses. In the distance, she could hear the whine of a lawnmower but apart from that there were no other signs of habitation. Fleetby-on-the-Hill was too quiet, Jade decided; she'd be glad to get back to Trafalgar Road.

At the post box outside Mrs Lunn's shop, she glanced at the envelopes and hesitated. Mr Cooper's letter could go, she decided, and so could Jacob's. They were slipped into the mouth of the letter box without a second thought, but her invitation to have Rosie and Navid sleep over for a few days seemed to stick to her warm palm. What if they didn't want to come because of Goran? Maybe Mrs Haldijary wouldn't think she was a suitable friend? On the other hand, what if they came and were bored stiff? Navid had to be active all the time. How would he survive without a computer and Sky TV?

Sadly, she folded the envelope in half and slid it into her pocket. She needed more time to think about it. Maybe it would be better if she waited until September, when they were all at the High School as equals, to renew her friendship with them.

Turning, she started slowly back down the main street. Still reluctant to go back to the cottage just yet, Jade paused by the church gate. To distract herself, she began to read the notice board. Mrs Lunn was on the flower rota for July and August, apparently, and the Mother and Toddler group wouldn't be meeting again until October when the new cushion-flooring had been laid in the church hall. Navid's voice boomed in her ear. *Fetch a paramedic—the excitement is killing me!* She had been right not to post the letter.

Jade glanced through the wrought iron fretwork at the marble grave beyond, remembering Mrs Lunn's story about Wilfred Whitehead. Might as well check out the inscription, she thought as she entered the churchyard.

The inscription was simple, for such an elaborate grave. *Here lies Wilfred Whitehead, born 1918 died 1979 squire of Fleetby Hall, Fleetby-on-the-Hill. Also Elizabeth Whitehead his wife born 1921 died 1990. At peace.*

At peace. Huh! That was a joke with Annie Hesketh hacking all over you, Jade thought. Serves you right, too. She was about to move on to the next grave when she heard the squeak, squeak, squeak of the old woman's pram as it was wheeled along the path.

Jade's first instinct was to walk away but it was too late. Miss Hesketh was level with her now, beginning her pacing to and fro at the foot of the grave, seemingly unaware of her neighbour watching her with intense curiosity. She was used to being stared at by strangers.

'Hello,' Jade began.

No reply. Jade stepped closer, slowly so as not to startle, and pretended to peer into the pram. 'That's a bonny baby,' she said soothingly. Miss Hesketh mumbled something. 'What a bonny baby,' Jade repeated, her heart pounding.

'Billy,' the old woman muttered, leaning forward to pull the hood of the battered contraption higher.

Jade, delighted to have got through to the old woman, reached out to help. 'Yes, you don't want him getting sun on his face. Billy, is it? That's a sweet name.'

'Billy,' Miss Hesketh repeated gruffly, her eyes darting towards Jade and back into the depths of the empty carriage.

Jade held her breath, wondering what to say next. What did you say, really? Before she could think of anything, she noticed small bubbles of saliva foaming at the corners of Miss Hesketh's mouth. Quickly, she took a step back, in case she was within firing range of the grave.

A stone rolled on to the path nearby, almost flicking Jade's ankle. 'Hey, you!' came an urgent whisper. Jade looked across to the gate where the red-haired girl she had seen around the village was beckoning frantically to her.

'Oh, hi!' Jade replied, pleased that she, too, was communicating. Smiling, she began to make her way through the long grass towards the stone-thrower.

The girl's eyes were opened wide in horror. 'Come away from her! That's Mad Annie. She'll stab you!'

'No she won't!' Jade laughed, astounded at the

suggestion. Annie wouldn't be able to hold a butter knife in her arthritic fingers, let alone make a stab with it.

But her would-be rescuer was adamant. 'She will! She's a witch—ask anyone. She kills cats and eats dog dirt and all sorts. You shouldn't go anywhere near.'

Jade nodded understandingly—after all, she'd thought the same until recently. All the girl needed was to hear the explanation, to find out the reason, then she'd understand. 'She's just old and a bit potty but she's harmless. Haven't you heard her story from Mrs Lunn?'

The girl frowned sourly. 'No, and I don't want to. My mum says Mad Annie's a Bellwood Loony and I've to stay well away and so should you, if you've got any sense!'

Jade felt herself growing angry and hot. She thought of the young Annie, locked away in a hospital for years and then being freed, only to have to face abuse and name-calling for the rest of her life, just for being different. Just for being one in seven. She thought of Molly's contemptuous neighbours twitching their net curtains and gawping at her. Most of all, she thought of her father's face that afternoon, so tired from his treatment. She thought of the effort he was making to get better and how difficult it was for all of them knowing he never would. Their world was hard enough without stupid people making it harder.

Advancing furiously towards the girl, Jade almost shouted her reply. 'Is that right? Mad Annie's a Bellwood Loony, is she? Well, for your information my dad's a "Bellwood Loony" too, but so what? It's not their fault!' she yelled.

For Jade, the admission of her father's illness was like a thunderbolt but she didn't regret it one tiny bit. In fact, it made her feel relieved. Better than relieved. It made her feel strong, like Molly. Her breathing quickened as she waited for the girl's reaction. If the girl insulted her father, she'd thump her, she decided. The girl looked at Jade askance, clearly not believing her. 'I'm only trying to do you a favour. It's not my fault if you've got a death wish.'

Jade's head dropped and her anger dissolved like sugar in hot tea. Getting het up wasn't going to solve anything. She needed to be patient. Honest and patient. 'I haven't got a death wish. Come in and talk to her with me. Ask her about her baby.'

'Billy,' Miss Hesketh grunted.

But the girl's mouth had set in to a mean, hard line. 'You're thick for talking to her. She'll get you, then you'll be sorry.'

'I know you shouldn't talk to strangers,' Jade began, 'and some mental people are dangerous but not most of them. My dad would never hurt a fly and Miss Hesketh's had an awful—'

She wasn't allowed to finish.

'I was going to ask you if you wanted to hang out but I'm not now,' the girl stated haughtily. 'You're mad, you are!' With that, she mounted her bike, shooting Jade a look of pure venom.

She stared after the girl, following her with puzzled eyes as she cycled furiously away in the distance. *You're mad, you are!* The words rang in Jade's ears. How different the phrase sounded this time compared to the way Molly had said it in the shop yesterday. *You're mad, you are.*

Jade shrugged her shoulders. She knew she wasn't mad. The girl had only reacted how Grandma had warned her she would with silly name-calling. People were just scared, she realized. Scared of the symptoms, like she had been. Scared of what they didn't understand.

Jade back-heeled a stone into a clump of grass. Not everybody was like that, though. When Goran was ranting and raving in the street, some of the people had jeered but not all of them. Some had been kind and sympathetic. Navid wouldn't have made fun. And there was no way Rosie would have, either. She was filled with shame that she had even thought they would not have been on her side. Not for the first time recently, she wished she had seen the end of term out with them.

Maybe news of Goran's breakdown in Trafalgar Road would have made it back to school; maybe a few kids would have made sly comments at her expense, but her real friends wouldn't.

Still, she only knew that now, weeks later, standing in this overgrown graveyard near to Wilfred Whitehead's betrayed fiancée. Besides, if she had attended the service, she would never have met Molly, and meeting Molly had changed her life.

From close behind came the unmistakable sound of Wilfred and Elizabeth being zealously pelted with spittle. 'You go, girl!' she encouraged the old woman before striding back to the postbox.

17

'Is my tie OK, Dad?' Jade asked nervously.

Goran furrowed his eyebrows and nodded. 'It's as it should be.'

'Right then, I'd better go downstairs and have my photo taken with Nav and Rosie before Mum gets even more stressed out. Are you going to come?'

As she had expected, Goran shook his head. Although he was home now, and much better, he was still tired and preferred to stay upstairs in the flat, away from any fuss. Hurriedly, Jade gathered her schoolbag, feeling a rush of excitement as she remembered Molly in Big Fat Zero all those weeks ago. She turned and smiled at her father. 'Any advice for me on my first day?' she asked.

'Be neat,' her father replied from the depths of his newspaper.

'OK, I'll be neat,' Jade said and dashed out to join her friends.

She arrived outside the front of Inks to find Navid already acting up.

'No, no, move to the left, to the left, Navid, and face me!' Ruth instructed him, one hand flapping wildly at him, the other trying to hold the camera steady. Jade went to stand between the twins, just in case.

'That boy!' Jacob chortled as he swept the pavement outside the bakery.

Navid reluctantly stopped looking at his reflection in Inks's shop window and smiled charmingly. 'Can't you just take one of me on my own, Mrs Winter? These two are just too ugly to be seen with someone so cool!'

'You're not cool. I've seen cooler things in one of Dad's hankies!' Rosie said, stretching across to claw her brother's arm.

'Pack it in, you guys. We haven't even got on the bus yet and you've started,' Jade protested, posing for the camera.

'Put your bag down, Jade, I can't see your face,' Ruth moaned.

'And the problem with that is?' Navid asked.

Jade lowered the bag slightly. She wanted it to feature prominently for when she sent copies of the photographs to Molly in her next letter.

'OK, one more and then I'll let you go,' Ruth said, her voice wavering. They looked so smart, so grown-up. She clicked and sighed. 'Right, then. I suppose you're too old for a kiss now?' she said, addressing her daughter.

Jade was busy showing off her new watch, a present from her grandma, and didn't hear. Ruth repeated her request. 'Yo! Secondary School Kid! Hug—now!'

'If I have to,' Jade teased, surrendering herself to her mother's outstretched arms.

'You'll be OK, won't you?' Ruth whispered as she squeezed Jade tightly.

'If I don't die of suffocation first,' Jade protested. Glancing over her mother's shoulder she caught sight of Goran's reflection in the window. 'Dad's in the shop,' Jade hissed in Ruth's ear.

'Really?'

'Really.'

'That's progress. He's come to see you off.'

'Maybe,' Jade agreed, 'but he's been side-tracked.'

Goran was staring bewilderedly at the desk they'd brought from Church Cottage. Jade saw him tentatively touch the roll top, his hand sliding slowly down the convex as if he were stroking a sleeping cat. A smile crossed his lips and the expression on his face changed. It was as if he had found something that at last made sense to him.

The desk had been in Inks for over a fortnight now. Jade hadn't been able to bear it when Rob had come to collect it for the auction rooms so she had persuaded Ruth to buy it from him. They had haggled for ages over the price and Jade had thrown in her fifty pounds worth of gift vouchers which had clinched the deal and shut them both up.

It fitted perfectly in the shop. Ruth thought it would make a good display piece for the window but Jade thought it should be further back, so people could sit at it and test the pens at a genuine writing desk. In the end they had left the purchase in the middle of the floor, waiting for Goran to decide.

'What's he doing now?' Ruth asked.

'Opening it.'

'Do you think he likes it?'

'Yes.'

'Thank goodness!'

'Mrs Winter?' Navid interrupted. 'Can we have our friend back now, please. We want to get to the bus stop before everyone nicks the best seats.'

'First she has to give me a hug, too!' Jacob said gruffly.

'You're a right sloppy lot on Trafalgar Road, you are,' Navid scoffed as Jade embraced Mr Krazinski. 'Look, there's a bloke coming out of the newsagent's. Why don't you go and snog him and all, Jade?'

'Navid, you know I love only you, my sweetheart,' Jade taunted, advancing towards the boy with lips puckered.

'Get lost, you sex-starved beast!' Navid protested, bolting down the street.

'Works every time! High five, Jade!' Rosie laughed.

The two friends smacked hands mid-air and bolted after him.

Other books by Helena Pielichaty

Simone's Letters

ISBN 0 19 275087 9

*Dear Mr Cakebread . . . For starters my name is Simone, not Simon
. . . Mum says you sound just like my dad. My dad, Dennis, lives in
Bartock with his girlfriend, Alexis . . . My mum says lots of rude
things about her because Alexis was one of the reasons my parents got
divorced (I was the other) . . .*

When ten-year-old Simone starts writing letters to Jem
Cakebread, the leading man of a touring theatre company, she
begins a friendship that will change her life . . . and the lives
of all around her: her mum, her best friend Chloe, her new
friend Melanie—and not forgetting Jem himself!

This collection of funny and often touching letters charts Simone's
final year at Primary School; from a school visit to *Rumpelstiltskin's
Revenge* to her final leaving Assembly; through the ups and downs
of her friendships—and those of her mum and dad.

Simone's Diary

ISBN 0 19 271842 8

*Dear Mr Cohen . . . Hi, it's me, Simone Anna Wibberley. Do you
remember me from when you were a student on teaching practice with
Miss Cassidy's class? . . . I am applying to be in your experiment . . .
I will answer everything as fully as I can . . . I am quite good at this
sort of thing because I used to fill in a lot of questionnaires in
magazines with my dad's ex-girlfriend, Alexis . . .*

Simone has left Woodhill Primary School behind her and is
starting life at her new secondary school. It's a little bit scary and
there are lots of new things to get used to, so when she's asked
to start writing a diary about her new experiences at Bartock
High School, it's the perfect opportunity for Simone to write
down all her thoughts and ideas in her own inimitable style.

Vicious Circle

ISBN 0 19 275113 1

'Why haven't we got any money? We've never got any money. Why can't we be like other people and have fish and chips when we fancy?'

Ten-year-old Louisa May and her mother Georgette are two of the 'have-nots', shuttling between ever-seedier bed and breakfast accommodation. To help cope with this way of life they play elaborate fantasy games, pretending to be the characters in the romantic fiction that Georgette borrows from the library in every town they move to.

When they arrive at the Cliff Top Villas Hotel in a run-down seaside resort and Georgette falls ill, it looks as if the fantasy will have to end. But Louisa May enlists the help of Joanna, another hotel resident, and together they determine to find out the truth behind Georgette's 'let's pretend' existence. Maybe this way there will be a chance for them to break out of the vicious circle and become 'haves' at last . . .

Getting Rid of Karenna

ISBN 0 19 271819 3

It was happening again and I felt as hopeless and stupid as ever. When you were scared, you were scared and nothing could take away that sick, twisted feeling you got in the pit of your stomach, no matter how old you were.

Even now Suzanne can remember the fear, the humiliation, the pain, caused by the constant bullying; the two year reign of terror in which she had been driven to the brink of a breakdown. It is three years since Karenna left the school and Suzanne is beginning to put it all behind her, but suddenly Karenna has come back into her life. Is it all going to begin again? Will she never be free of the nightmare? In order to get on with her own life, Suzanne has to find some way to rid herself of the past . . . of Karenna.

'This is it, Louisa May.'

Louisa May nodded. 'I thought it might be.'

'Cliff Top Villas Hotel. Isn't it splendid? Just as we'd imagined.'

'Better. Look at the pretty garden full of flowers and all the rooms have their own balcony. We'll be able to sit outside and watch the sun set over the sea.'

'We're going to have a lovely holiday here, I just know it.'

'I hope so, Mama, we deserve a treat.'

'You are so right.'

Georgette swooped to kiss the top of her daughter's head. 'There's probably a butler called Perkins and a chambermaid called Sally-Anne waiting inside. They'll be drinking China tea and eating homemade seed cake while they muse about us, their important guests.'

Louisa May sighed. She was tired now and her tight shoes had rubbed blisters on her heels after the walk up the steep hill. She struggled to release her two carrier bags which had entwined themselves into her fingers like plastic creepers. Cliff Top Villas Hotel was a dump.

There was no front garden, only a concreted forecourt enclosed by a low breeze-block wall. Discarded polystyrene food-trays, streaked with curry stains, gathered forlornly in damp corners. Louisa May quickly surveyed the front of the hotel, with its paint-starved woodwork and filthy bay windows, its lopsided 'vacancies' sign thrust against drab, grey, net curtains. She knew the best they could hope for was a lavatory that flushed.

Georgette peered uncertainly at the row of buttons which sprouted from the inside of the doorway, fumbling to release her own carrier bags and therefore the rest of all they owned, so she could ring the bell.

Louisa May turned from the house and gazed across the road. For the first time that day, her spirits rose. On the long walk up Cliff Bank, head down against the wind, eyes fixed on Georgette's purple boots, she hadn't seen the houses give way to clumps of sand-clogged grass that marked a boundary between road and cliff-edge. Nor had she been aware of the choppy sea sparkling in the bay beneath. It looked wonderful.

She hadn't wanted to move this time. She'd liked living in Lincoln, even if it had only been in a squat behind the crisp factory. She'd liked the swans on the river and the cold peace that filled her inside the cathedral. And the Social had promised a place of their own, in time. But then the letters had arrived, and for once Georgette had been quick and decisive. They had to leave. Again.

Louisa May had cried and made her mother choose somewhere nice, like the seaside. So here they were, somewhere along the east coast, in an unknown resort called Wathsea. Waiting.

'Yeah?'

The voice was deep and gruff. Louisa May spun round immediately and stood at her mother's side, where she knew she'd be needed.

Georgette cleared her throat. 'Good afternoon, Mr Putlock, I'm Mrs Van Der Lees and this is my daughter, Louisa May. I believe you are expecting us? My agent made a reservation on our behalf earlier today for a double room with all facilities.'

She smiled politely at the man staring rudely at her, appearing not to notice he was only wearing a bath towel tied loosely round his flabby middle and that water dripped in dark streams down his hairy legs.

136

'I was in the bath,' he grumbled.

'If you could kindly show us to our room, we are both in urgent need of refreshing ourselves before we dine,' Louisa May's mother continued.

The man scratched at the flesh beneath the towel. 'What are you on about?'

Louisa May sighed. Georgette had forgotten to go back to normal again. Forgotten that people didn't play pretend like they did. She'd have to do the talking. She hated having to do the talking.

'Erm . . . Mrs Chambers sent us . . . she said she'd telephoned to check it was all right . . . that you did rooms for people like us.'

A look of dislike flicked over the man's face. 'Chambers? That mardy piece from the Social, you mean?' Louisa May nodded, as if agreeing with him, although she'd liked Mrs Chambers. Mrs Chambers had been kind, speaking patiently to Georgette and giving them tea and chocolate marshmallows. They didn't usually do that. Perhaps everyone was kinder at the seaside.

'Young man, our room, please.' Georgette arched her left eyebrow expressively. Her feet were beginning to ache too.

'Now just hang on a minute you, with your young man and rooms with all facilities. I've told them down there before: no kids, no druggies, and no weirdos. You're all three by the looks of it.'

'Quite. Standards are so important. Now is there a porter to attend to our luggage?'

'Mum,' Louisa May pleaded in a small voice.

'Yes, dear?'

'Let's not play the game until we get inside.'

'Try not to interrupt while I'm dealing with the proprietor, darling. We mustn't appear to be rude, must we?'

137

The half-naked proprietor snorted. 'Hey, Wanda,' he shouted over his shoulder into the dark hallway. He waited a few seconds. 'Wanda! Come and sort this lot out.'

There was a stone in Louisa May's left shoe. She could feel it jabbing through her sock. She couldn't wait for tomorrow. Tomorrow she could have some new shoes. New shoes that didn't squash her feet and make her toes burn like the ones she was wearing. New shoes from a proper shoe shop.

The door opened further. A woman with yolk-yellow hair piled high on top of her head emerged. The hair was pulled back so tightly it seemed to stretch her face along with it, making it seem pinched and plucked.

'What's up now? You know I'm doing me nails for tonight.' She held her freshly painted talons in front of her face, pleased with the results.

'Sort these two out before I freeze to death. They're from the Social.'

Once again, Louisa May felt the sting of cold eyes judging her.

'You're not New Age, are you? We don't want none of them, with their mucky dogs and mucky habits.'

'I've already told them that. She's not right, that one. Another loony to add to the pack. We'll have a full set soon if we don't watch it.' The man scowled at Georgette before disappearing inside.

Wanda scratched her shoulder. She looked searchingly at Georgette, who was fanning her face against an imagined heat. In their game, it was the height of summer, not the end of October.

Louisa May shuffled awkwardly. She knew her mother appeared odd, in her baggy jumpers and thin skirts layered over and over each other like bun cases, but the more you wore, the less you carried. It made things easier when travelling. She wished Georgette hadn't draped that mangy fox-fur round her neck, though, or stuck glass beads and hat pins at all angles through her black hat. It made her look like a little girl playing at dressing-up.

Wanda was staring at Louisa May now; staring at her spindly legs and charity shop clothes, at her gritty uncut hair and pale thin face. 'Have you got your giro?' she demanded.

'Yes. Mrs Chambers gave it to us.'

Wanda shrugged. 'You can come in then, but remember it's only temp'ry. Come April, you're out. We only take in your lot from the Social to tide us through the winter. Nobody comes to Wathsea in winter. There's nothing to come for.' She paused, as if waiting to be contradicted, but they had already passed through the town, with its desolate sea-front and dilapidated hotels. The only surprise was that people came at all.

'Do you think it would be possible to show us to our room now? We do seem to have been waiting a dreadfully long time.' It was Georgette in her 'dealing-with-the-servants' voice. Louisa May grimaced. She lifted her eyes cautiously to see how the landlady would react.

Wanda's dark eyebrows narrowed. 'Oh, I do beg your pardon, your ladyship, whatever can I 'ave been thinking of? Do come in and allow me to escort you to your room. And I do apologize for the lacking of the red carpet but one of the queen's corgis did a poopy on it on their last visit and it's not beck from the dry cleaners yet.'

Louisa May's face burned as she followed her mother indoors. Come April you're out, Eggy-hair had said. If they lasted a week it would be a miracle.

* * *

139

Their room was at the far end of the dingy second-floor landing. A familiar smell of damp and dogs clung to the stale air. To Louisa May, houses like this always smelt of dogs, even when there weren't any.

'Right, here we are then, the Royal Suite,' Wanda continued in her fake posh voice. She opened the door ceremoniously, allowing Georgette to lead the way.

They had lived in worse places. At least the wallpaper wasn't peeling off and there was glass in the windows, unlike their basement room in Lincoln. Their two divan beds were draped in lurid orange coverlets, separated by a cheap, laminated dressing table. The curtains were too short for the window, the carpet too long for the room. It curled up at each end like stale toast.

Wanda began to fire instructions at them. 'The toilet's at the end of the landing. Provide your own paper. No cooking in your room but there is coffee and tea making facilities. You'll need fifty pences for the electric. Breakfast's between seven and eight-thirty sharp. Ambrose and me don't cash cheques or lend money or stand for late payments. If you was proper guests it'd be different but me and Ambrose have found it best to let people like you keep yourselves to yourselves.' Wanda spoke directly to Louisa May, who nodded.

'And bathing arrangements?' Georgette enquired, as she slowly plucked off her evening gloves, a finger at a time.

'Bathing arrangements?' asked Wanda, watching the much-practised routine with curiosity.

'I notice our room is not en-suite.'

'You'll also notice it's not the 'ilton, neither. You've got a sink and there's a bath next to the toilet. Beggars can't be choosers, you know!'

Louisa May stiffened. They might be homeless but they had never begged yet. Georgette carefully laid down her gloves on the bed.

'Very well. That will be all, Mrs Putlock.'

'Not quite all, Mrs . . . ?'

'Mrs Van Der Lees.'

'Mrs Vandaleese? Very posh. Foreign, is it?'

'Dutch.'

'Thought so. We get a lot of foreigners staying here. Stands to reason. No state handouts where they come from, is there?'

'Was there anything else?' Georgette asked.

'Just your giro to sort out.'

'Giro?' Georgette sounded as though it was something she'd never heard of in her life instead of something that had helped her through the past nine years. Wanda watched Georgette's reaction closely. Something in her eyes flickered then changed.

'The . . . er . . . docket Mrs Chambers gave you down at the Social. I can deal with it for you; it'd be no bother. Save you all that inconvenience of having to queue up with those rough types you get down there. A lady like you doesn't want to have to do that.' Wanda's voice was silky-smooth without a trace of the earlier mockery.

'It would save me a lot of time and allow my daughter and I the chance to become acclimatized to our surroundings,' Georgette agreed.

'Dead right. You get your feet up—rest them pretty ankles.'

Georgette unclipped her sequined evening bag, and began to sort carefully through its contents.

'Now, let me see where I placed it.'

'I like to help whenever I can,' Wanda said. She was almost pleasant now, smiling down at Louisa May. Louisa May didn't smile back. She knew her game.

Wanda's eyes brightened as Georgette withdrew a brown envelope from her bag.

'Just sign it at the back, love. That gives me permission to cash it, as your agent. I do it for most of the residents.'

'Certainly, and as you have been so helpful I wish you to take a shilling from the change, to compensate you for your trouble.' Georgette signed the cheque with a flourish and handed it over to Wanda. Wanda glanced briefly at the amount shown on the cheque and her mouth puckered greedily. Anger surged through Louisa May like a stab of hunger. She knew there was extra money on the cheque, a clothing allowance for when she started at her new school. Georgette was going to hand over all the money they had to this horrible witch with yellow hair. They'd never see any of it.

'Mum,' Louisa May's voice faltered.

'Not now, dear.'

'Mum.'

'Not now, dear. It's rude to interrupt.'

'But, Mum, Mrs Chambers said to cash it yourself. She told you twice.'

Wanda interrupted swiftly. 'Oh, her. Doesn't know a thing, if you ask me.'

'Well, nobody is asking you, are they?' Louisa May burst out.

'Louisa May! How dare you be so disrespectful! Apologize at once to Mrs Putlock!' Two bright pink spots flared against Georgette's hollow cheeks as she stared in dismay at her daughter.

Louisa May glared stubbornly at the bitty, turquoise carpet. Wanda sniffed. 'Kids, eh? They've got that much lip. I'm glad me and Ambrose never had any.' She carefully folded the brown envelope and slipped it into her pocket.

'If you could leave us now, Mrs Putlock,' Georgette asked politely.

142

'Right you are. I'll go cash this for you. It should just about cover two weeks board and lodgings.' The landlady closed the door behind her, leaving a faint odour of cigarettes and sweat. Louisa May threw herself down on to the nearest bed and sank her face into the orange cover. It smelt of cat pee.

'Louisa May, whatever have I done to deserve this behaviour?' Georgette asked in a concerned voice.

'Beggars can't be choosers,' Louisa May answered, curling herself into a tight ball.

* * *

Louisa May must have fallen asleep because when she awoke the room was darker. Her mother was sitting upright against the headrest of her bed, reading. She had already unpacked her own things. The three carrier bags were folded in neat squares on the dressing table.

Steam arose from the sink, misting the cracked blue tiles above it. That would be their underwear soaking. Washing their pants and socks was always the first thing Georgette did when they arrived in a new place. They didn't have enough knickers to allow them to stockpile and sometimes they had to share.

'Is there anything to eat?' Louisa May asked. Georgette didn't hear her. Once she started reading, she entered another world. Her books were stacked beside her bed in three knee-high columns. Each pile a carrier bag full.

'Mum!' Louisa May repeated. 'Mum!'

'Mmm?' Georgette asked, turning a page.

'I'm hungry.'

'Get something to eat then.'

'What?'

'Whatever you want.'

'OK. I'll ring Perkins and ask him to bring me a pizza, shall I?' Georgette dragged her eyes away from her book, smiling as Louisa May, pretending her hand was a telephone, spoke poshly into the 'receiver'. 'Hello, room service? I'd like a very, very large pizza, please, with tons of cheese. And fifteen bottles of Coca Cola. No, not Diet Coke, real Coke. Room five, please. That's right, the Van Der Lees apartment, at the double. Thank you.' She 'hung up'. 'Van Der Lees! Where did you dig that one up from?' Georgette tapped the cover of the book she was reading. Louisa May bent forward to see what it said. *The Temptations of Rosanna Van Der Lees.* She groaned. 'Not her again.'

'She's great. I've almost read the whole series. This is the last one.'

Louisa May raised her eyes to the ceiling. 'Thank you, God.'

Georgette began to quote from the book. ' "Rosanna sighed as the scent of honeysuckle drifted towards her from the garden below. If only Gilbert were here to share her bliss." ' Georgette paused dreamily. 'Isn't that wonderful? Can't you just smell that honeysuckle?'

'I can't smell anything except your feet. It's daft, like all the stuff you read. Daft and soppy.'

'It's daft! It's daft!' Georgette threw the book down and leapt off the bed. She lunged at Louisa May who screeched as she tried to dodge Georgette's dangerous fingers.

'Don't! Don't!' Louisa May shrieked with excitement, trying to struggle free. This was more like it. Her mother, dressed in her old leggings and tatty jumper, playing and being silly. After a while, Georgette sat back on her bed, breathless from their play-acting. Louisa May tried again with the food.

'Really though, can't we go downstairs and see what time dinner's ready?' she pleaded.

The light died in her mother's eyes. Georgette fastened a strand of lank hair behind her ear and sighed heavily, as if all her energy had been squeezed out of her in one long breath. 'You go, I'll rinse out the smalls and finish unpacking.'

'I don't want to go on my own.'

'You'll be all right.' Georgette crossed over to the sink and began half-heartedly pumping the wet clothes around, her thin shoulder blades as sharp as shark fins through her worn jumper. 'I'm not hungry.'

Louisa May traced a circle on the bedcover with her finger, running round and round it with her nail.

'Why did you give that woman all our money?' she asked quietly.

Georgette stopped washing for a second.

'She'll bring it back.'

'How do you know?' Louisa May persisted. Her mother was usually so careful with their money; it had been a shock to see her hand over the giro so readily. Georgette squeezed out a pair of socks and set them down against the splashback, turned and smiled.

'She'll bring it back, I promise.'

Louisa May's stomach growled painfully before she could answer.

'You'd better find that pizza,' Georgette ordered.

Outside the room, the landing was dark and narrow. Louisa May hurried down the stairs then stopped at the bottom. There were a number of doors leading off from the draughty hallway. The one furthest away was closed, with 'Private' written at the top. Next to it were two more doors, both slightly ajar. One of these would be the dining room, the other the lounge. That was the usual set-up in these places. She hoped the evening meal was the sort where you helped yourself. If so, she'd just grab whatever there was and take it back upstairs.

Louisa May sniffed. She could smell fried fish. Fish and chips were her favourite. Happily, she pushed open the door and wondered whether there'd be seconds. But it wasn't the dining room she entered, only the lounge. There were fish and chips but they were being eaten out of a crater of grease-soaked newspaper by a woman sitting in an armchair. She looked up guiltily when Louisa May entered and paused with a chip half-way to her mouth.

'Oh,' she said and ate the chip hurriedly. Louisa May stood in the doorway, not sure what to do. The woman smiled and pointed to her fish and chips. 'Will you help me finish these? I'll never get rid of them before they go cold.'

Louisa May shook her head. Hungry as she was, she knew not to take food from strangers. 'I'm waiting for the evening meal,' she said.

The woman took a swig from a can of Coke at her feet.

'Huh! I wouldn't bother if I were you.'

'Why?'

'Well, A, you'll have to wait until seven o'clock and B, the food is revolting.'

Louisa May's stomach growled loudly. 'I can't wait until then. It's only five o'clock now!'

'Have some chips, then. You can see I shouldn't be eating all these calories,' the woman offered, patting her rounded stomach. Louisa May didn't move. Keen eyes probed hers. 'You do right to refuse, though I promise I'm harmless. Where's your mum and dad?'

'My mum's upstairs.'

'Oh.' The woman set down the fish and chips on the chair beside her. Louisa May reckoned she looked like a coconut. She was definitely as oval as one but it was the hair that did it; although it was short at the sides, a stubborn, ginger tuft sprouted proudly skywards from the crown just like a coconut's. The coconut grinned.

'Welcome to Putlock's Palace. I'm Joanna Frankish, room four.'

'That's the room next to us. I'm Louisa May.'

'Louisa May? Not plain old Louisa?'

'No. Louisa May. After Louisa May Alcott, who wrote *Little Women*.'

'Very posh. A bit long, though. Can I call you Lou instead?'

Louisa May shook her head again. 'My mum thinks it's vulgar to shorten names.'

'Oh, that's a shame. I think Lou's more . . . cute American kid.'

Louisa May beamed. She liked the idea. 'Well, gee thanks, ma'am.'

Joanna laughed, a crackling laugh that made her chin wobble. 'What if I just call you Lou when we're by ourselves? So, have you got any brothers or sisters, Lou? Any Enids or Roalds?'

'No, there's just me and my mum. She's called Georgette.'

'Don't tell me. After Georgette Heyer, writer of historical romantic fiction, right?'

'Right.'

'My nan's got all hers. Hey, your dad's not called Charles Dickens by any chance?'

'No, Daniel Brody,' Louisa May smiled. Joanna seemed friendly and she had a nice way of talking, like the pretty lady on *Blue Peter*. Perhaps she could be trusted with The Story.

'The nurse who found my mum was reading a book by

147

Georgette Heyer and that's why they named her Georgette.'

'Found her?'

Louisa May nodded and sidled further into the room but still keeping a distance between them. She loved telling this. 'Yes. When she was a new-born baby my mum was left in a hospital dustbin and nearly died.' It had actually been a corridor outside the baby-care unit but Louisa May thought a dustbin was more dramatic.

'A dustbin? I know cuts in the health service are bad but that's taking things a bit too far. Did anyone find out who left her there?'

Louisa May continued solemnly. 'No. My mum was brought up in a children's home and nobody there knew anything. But last year a woman called Wendy Almond started writing to us, which is strange because we never get letters. My mum says that must be her mum trying to find her because that's what women do when they've let their babies be adopted. They wait until you're all grown up then come looking for you to say sorry but Wendy Almond can get lost because we're not interested. In fact, mum says she doesn't want to see her until she's on her death bed and then only to spit in her eye!'

Joanna looked surprised at the girl's anger but replied evenly, 'Good for her. Still, I suppose this Wendy Almond must have had her reasons.'

'Mum says there can't be any reasons for abandoning your own child. She hates even talking about it. They tried to take me into care once but she wouldn't let them.'

Joanna drained her can. She looked with renewed interest at the young girl in front of her. 'Why don't you sit down. Tell me all about yourself? I bet you've had a fascinating life.'

Louisa May bit her lip. She'd gone too far already. 'We're just normal, like everyone else.'

'Of course you are, everyone I know was born in a dustbin!'

'Not born in a dustbin, found in a dustbin,' Louisa May corrected.

'Sorry, found in a dustbin.'

'We're just normal.'

'So you said. Are you sure you won't sit down? It's not much but it's home!' Joanna joked. Louisa May looked around. It was a dingy room with a huge wooden sideboard pushed against the chimney breast. Around this huddled five dilapidated armchairs facing a dust-covered television set.

Joanna's eyes followed hers. 'No use looking at that thing, it's broken. One of the previous residents thought he was a surgeon and took all its insides out. It's a laugh a minute in this place, girl.'

Louisa May's heart sank. She liked television. Joanna stood up and pushed the fish paper down the side of the chair.

'How long have you been here?' Louisa May asked.

'Since the end of June when I left university with a Geography degree but without a job. I worked in a rock factory during the summer but it was only seasonal and I've just stayed on. This place kind of suits my mood.'

Louisa May gazed longingly at the broken television, not really listening. 'What do you do at night if there's no telly?' she asked, more to herself than Joanna.

Joanna hesitated. 'I have a TV in my room. You can watch that whenever you want to. It'll be nice to have company other than woodlice and spiders. I warn you, though, I'm allergic to anything Australian.'

'Honest? I can watch whenever I want? That's cool. I'll have to ask my mum first.'

The television owner rummaged around in her shoulder bag. 'Here, cop this.' She threw an apple towards Louisa

149

May who caught it against her chest. 'And these.' A packet of peanuts was lobbed in the same direction. 'Emergency rations, for those at peril on the sea or kids named after famous writers.'

'Thanks, Coconut.' The nickname slipped out without thinking. Joanna patted her spiky hair and giggled.

'Well, I've been called worse!'

Louisa May returned happily to her room, glad to have met someone nice at the hotel.

* * *

When Louisa May bounced into their room, she found her mother crying. Large, bulbous tears ran freely down her cheeks.

'What's wrong, Mum?'

'He's dead, Louisa May, he's dead.'

'Who?'

'Gilbert.'

'Gilbert?'

'Gilbert Farthingale, Rosanna's fiancé. He's been killed in a duel.'

'Oh, is that all?'

'It's so cruel. Her first fiancé died of cholera, her second died saving a child from drowning, and now poor Gilbert.'

'She should choose them better.'

'It's so, so sad.'

'Someone gave me an apple and some peanuts.'

Georgette looked up immediately.

'Who?' she asked sharply.

'A woman called Joanna Frankish. She looks like a coconut and eats a lot.'

'Oh, well, wash it first.' Louisa May rinsed the apple, noting their underwear was still in the sink.

'There's no food until seven o'clock so can we go and get some fish and chips?'

'We've no money until tomorrow.'

Louisa May tutted. It was always the same.

'Why haven't we got any money? We've never got any money. Why can't we be like other people and have fish and chips when we fancy?'

Her mother continued to read but replied calmly. 'We're not other people, Louisa May, and we've been over this a thousand times. To have money you have to have a job. To have a job you need somewhere to live. If you want to live somewhere you have to have money. I haven't got a job so we haven't got any money. Because we have no money we haven't got a house. We are the ''have-nots'' of this world.'

Louisa May nodded at this well-worn phrase. 'It'd be different if Dad was here, wouldn't it? We'd have a proper house then, wouldn't we?'

Georgette frowned, bending the spine of her book back irritably. 'If you say so.'

Louisa May knew these conversations never got her anywhere but she persisted in them anyway. 'He's been at sea since before I was born. He must be due a break by now. Even Captain Bligh came home in the end.' Sea adventures were the only stories she ever read willingly. Her observation fell on deaf ears. 'Tell me about him,' she pleaded.

'You know all there is to know,' Georgette muttered.

'Tell me anyway.'

'Your father's name was Daniel Brody. He was brought up in the same home as I was but we never spoke to each other until we were sixteen . . . '

'Because you were both too shy.'

'Then, a week before I was supposed to leave the home . . . '

151

'Because you were nearly seventeen and too old to stay.'

'He left a red rose on top of a book I was reading . . . '

' . . . *Rebecca* by Daphne Du Maurier.'

Georgette scowled. 'Who's telling the story here?' Louisa May sat upright and pulled a pretend zip across her mouth, allowing her mother to continue. 'Then, the night before I had to leave he knocked quietly on my bedroom door and when I answered he kissed me softly on the lips and said, "I will always love you." The next day I learned he had run away to sea, never to return. That kiss changed my life. A little while later I found out I was going to have a baby.'

'Me,' interrupted Louisa May.

'And because of this miracle I was allowed to stay on at the home until you were born.'

'Then they tried to take me away from you so you could finish your studies because you were brainy. I'm glad you didn't let them,' said Louisa May hotly.

Georgette stroked Louisa May's hair. 'Nobody will ever take you away, Louisa May. That's a promise.'

'I wish Wendy Almond hadn't left you.'

Georgette breathed in sharply. 'Why do you keep bringing her up?'

'Sorry.'

'The only time I want to see that woman is when?'

'When you're on your death bed so you can spit in her eye,' Louisa May chanted loyally. 'I know. I'm sorry.'

Georgette returned to her novel while Louisa May took a thoughtful bite from her apple. She was about to swallow when the whole room shook. Windows rattled and several books slid on to the carpet. Within seconds their door handle twisted and Mrs Wanda Putlock stormed into their room, thrusting a brown envelope at Georgette.

'Right you, Mrs Vanderleese from 'olland, I'm giving you one first and final warning. If you ever, ever, muck me around again you and that kid of yours are straight out on the street with all the other rubbish. Have you got that?'

Georgette hunched back on her bed and continued to read.

'I'm talking to you, lady!' Wanda screeched.

Georgette slowly looked up from her book. 'Does there seem to be a problem, Mrs Putlock?' she asked coolly.

Wanda almost growled her reply. 'Don't you Mrs Putlock me. I've never been so showed up in all my life when I tried to cash this with your false signature on it. Vanderleese, my foot. You're a Haddock!'

'By name if not by nature,' Georgette drawled.

'Don't you be clever with me, I'm warning you. Live in my house, live by my rules. Now I want my rent by lunchtime tomorrow or you are out of here. Is that clear?'

Georgette seemed immune to Wanda's anger. She yawned widely and picked up her book.

'And what's more,' Wanda continued, 'as you haven't paid for anything yet, you are not entitled to an evening meal, nor breakfast, so don't bother coming down for none until I see some money up front.'

'Your hospitality is overwhelming us, madam. Rarely have we received such a cordial welcome. Do close the door after you on the way out, there's a good servant.'

Wanda's eyes narrowed uncertainly. Georgette seemed to be serious. She was obviously unhinged. The landlady turned instead to Louisa May. 'I'd make that last if I were you,' she warned, staring at the uneaten apple in her hand. She tossed the envelope on to Louisa May's lap, then flounced out, leaving the door wide open.

Louisa May finally chewed the pulpy apple in her mouth. It was warm and tasteless and nearly impossible to swallow.

'I told you we'd get our money back,' Georgette stated, returning to Gilbert's funeral.

Other books by Helena Pielichaty

Vicious Circle
Simone's Letters
Simone's Diary
Getting Rid of Karenna

Jade's Story

Jade's face reddened as her father appeared in front of them . . .
He looked in such a state with his hair sticking up at all angles like
a mad professor's and his eyes glazed and staring, as if he were
drunk, though Jade knew he wasn't.

Jade doesn't know how to cope when her father starts
behaving oddly. He sits in a chair all day, staring into
space, not even bothering to get dressed—until Jade is too
embarrassed to bring her friends home. And then, to cap
it all, he wrecks his own shop, makes a scene in the
middle of the road, and has to be escorted off to hospital
by the police. Jade can't understand why her dad has to
behave like this. Why can't he be like other dads? Doesn't
he love her any more? It isn't until Jade realizes that her
dad isn't mad, but damaged by his past, that she can
understand his illness and help him get better.

Helena Pielichaty was born in Sweden to an English
mother and Polish-Russian father. Her family moved to
Yorkshire when Helena was five where she lived until
qualifying as a teacher from Bretton Hall College in 1978.
She has taught in various parts of the country including
East Grinstead, Oxford, and Sheffield. Helena now lives
with her husband, who is also half-Polish, in Nottingham-
shire where she divides her time between looking after
their two children, writing, teaching, and following the
trials and tribulations of Huddersfield Town A.F.C. *Jade's
Story* is her fourth novel for Oxford University Press.